Pranced

A Sierra Files Christmas Novella

By Christy Barritt

CHRISTY BARRITT

Pranced: A Novella
Copyright 2014 by Christy Barritt

Published by River Heights Press

Cover design by The Killion Group

This book is licensed for your personal enjoyment
only. Thank you for respecting the hard work of this
author.

The persons and events portrayed in this work are
the creation of the author, and any resemblance to
persons living or dead is purely coincidental.

CHRISTY BARRITT

Other Books by Christy Barritt

Squeaky Clean Mysteries:
#1 Hazardous Duty
#2 Suspicious Minds
#2.5 It Came Upon a Midnight Crime
#3 Organized Grime
#4 Dirty Deeds
#5 The Scum of All Fears
#6 To Love, Honor, and Perish
#7 Mucky Streak
#8 Foul Play
#9 Broom and Gloom
#10 Dust and Obey
#11 Thrill Squeaker
#11.5 Swept Away (a novella)
#12 Cunning Attractions
#13 Clean Getaway (coming soon)

The Sierra Files
#1 Pounced
#2 Hunted
#2.5 Pranced (a Christmas novella)
#3 Rattled
#4 Caged (coming soon)

The Gabby St. Claire Diaries (a tween mystery series)
#1 The Curtain Call Caper
#2 The Disappearing Dog Dilemma
#3 The Bungled Bike Burglaries

Holly Anna Paladin Mysteries
#1 Random Acts of Murder
#2 Random Acts of Deceit
#3 Random Acts of Malice
#3.5 Random Acts of Scrooge (a Christmas novella)
#4 Random Acts of Greed
#5 Random Acts of Fraud (coming soon)

The Worst Detective Ever
#1 Ready to Fumble
#2 Reign of Error
#3 Safety in Blunders

Carolina Moon series
#1 Home Before Dark
#2 Gone by Dark
#3 Wait Until Dark
#4 Light the Dark (a Christmas novella)

Suburban Sleuth Mysteries:
#1 Death of the Couch Potato's Wife

Romantic Suspense:
Keeping Guard
The Last Target
Race Against Time
Ricochet
Key Witness
Lifeline
High-Stakes Holiday Reunion
Desperate Measures

Hidden Agenda
Mountain Hideaway
Dark Harbor
Shadow of Suspicion

Romantic Mystery:
The Good Girl

Suspense:
Imperfect
Dubiosity
Disillusioned
Distorted (coming soon)

Nonfiction:
Changed: True Stories of Finding God through
Christian Music
The Novel in Me: The Beginner's Guide to Writing
and Publishing a Novel

Acknowledgements:

I'd like to thank Heather McCurdy, Deena Peterson, Chrystal Dodson, Jami Dillon, Angela Tanner, Sue Smith, and Chris Baker for their help with this manuscript.

CHAPTER 1

"Sierra! You're just as cute as I thought you'd be!" Chad's grandmother grabbed my cheeks and squeezed them like someone going gaga over a three year old. The problem was that I was closer to thirty than three. The other problem was that I had no choice but to smile through the I'm-the-new-girl-in-the-family ceremony. After all, I didn't want her first impression of me to be as someone who was difficult to get along with. She'd discover that soon enough.

"Thank you," I said, forcing a grin. His grandmother was exactly as I'd pictured her to be. She might look thin and frail, but her voice and her eyes said otherwise. She was petite with straight white hair that fell to her chin, and she smelled like roses.

I'd just driven six hours from Norfolk, Virginia to Oldsburgh, West Virginia where my husband Chad's aunt and uncle lived. The couple had invited us to spend Christmas with them, and we'd agreed.

Chad had arrived a day early to help out with some yard work. I'd insisted he go without me while I tidied things up at my office before taking four vacation days. It was one of the downsides to being the head honcho at a nonprofit—there was always work to be done.

At the moment, I stood in the cozy living room of his aunt and uncle's house. It was an oversized log cabin with a glowing fireplace and lots of natural light. The house smelled like evergreen and cinnamon and was decorated for Christmas, all the way down to the Santa hat perched on top of the mounted deer head above the mantle.

Or was that a reindeer head? I couldn't tell.

A grand Christmas tree so laden down with what appeared to be homemade ornaments that one could hardly see any green branches stood in the corner.

"Grandma, you're going to scare her," Chad said, putting his arm around my waist.

"But I'm just so happy you finally met someone." She turned her attention to Chad and squeezed his face together like it was silly putty now. "You're such a handsome young man, even with that rodent growing on your face."

"I'm happy, too, but muha pwhide . . . ."

Chad's lips were a scrunched up mess, making

most of his words unintelligible.

It was a tradition that his family gathered here every other year. The odd years, apparently, were reserved for the spouses' families. Anyway, Chad's family was everything mine wasn't: they were loud, boisterous, and warm.

My stomach had been in knots all week whenever I thought about this trip. I really wanted to make a good impression. Chad's family was important to him. I'd already met his mom and dad, but I hadn't met anyone else.

Thankfully, another woman swept onto the scene and distracted Grandma. "Sierra! You made it. Wonderful."

"You got here just in time." A round man with a round face, a full beard, and a gaudy Christmas apron emerged from the kitchen carrying a platter of colorful cookies.

"By the way, I'm Paula." His aunt had poofy blonde hair, a square face, boxy features, wore a Christmas turtleneck, and apparently liked green eye shadow and red lipstick. She also wore earrings inspired by gaudy Christmas light bulbs.

"And I'm Paul," his uncle said. "We know. It's strange."

"Even stranger, my maiden name was Davis also. Can you even imagine what a hoot our wedding was?" Aunt Paula slapped her leg and cackled with warm delight.

Chad had warned me about their names before we came, but insisted I let them take delight in telling me the story behind it. So I did. Stories were best told by the people who had lived them. That was my theory, at least.

"Anyway, the Davis family's annual Mountain Christmas Light Extravaganza starts tomorrow night," Aunt Paula said. "You got here just in time!"

I glanced at Chad and saw the guilt on his face. "Mountain Christmas Light Extravaganza?"

Chad shifted. "Did I not mention that? Well, we here in the Davis family have an annual Christmas light tradition."

"I gathered that," I deadpanned.

"I can't believe you didn't tell her about our Christmas light tradition, Chad," Aunt Paula said with a playful scoff.

"You see, my family pretty much owns this mountain," Chad said, pointing out the back window to the winter landscape that stretched upward toward the sky. "They decorate it with Christmas lights every year and people drive from miles around to see it."

"Why have you never told me this?"

He shrugged. "Didn't I? I thought I'd said

something about it when I mentioned coming early to help out."

"With yard work," I reminded him, keeping my voice light.

"All of the light work is in the *yard*. Therefore, I guess it is yard work. *P*otato po*tat*o, you know?"

As an unknown emotion passed through his gaze, my lips twisted in thought. I had a feeling he wasn't telling me something. We'd have to talk later.

"Anyway, we spent all day yesterday working on everything, and we're still not done," Chad said.

"Speaking of which, we need to assign everyone their tasks for the week," Aunt Paula said. "Sierra, we were hoping you'd be Mary."

I blinked, suddenly feeling out of sorts. "I'm sorry?"

"Mary, Mother of Jesus."

"For the light extravaganza," Uncle Paul explained.

"We thought it would be appropriate, especially since . . . you're expecting!" Aunt Paula squealed and pulled me into a hug.

Then grandmother pulled me into a hug.

Then Uncle Paul.

"We're just so happy for you both." Paula clasped her hands together and nestled them under her chin as she looked at Chad and I with adoration. "What a great Christmas surprise."

"One day, that baby of yours is going to love coming here to see our light display," Uncle Paul said, pride across his face.

"Don't let him fool you." Grandma waved her hand in the air. "It's more than a light display. It's a Christmas wonderland."

I nodded, feeling like I'd been sucked into a whirlwind, one filled with tinsel and fake snow and a whole lot of Christmas cheer. "I noticed there were a lot of decorations when I pulled up."

A lot would be an understatement. Their entire front yard had been filled with wooden decorations, plastic decorations, wire decorations, and lighted decorations.

You name it, Paul and Paula probably had it.

"We have a live nativity," Paula said. "We even have Santa!"

"I guess there's something for everyone then." I shifted, trying to comprehend all the new faces, the new ideas, and the unexpectedly busy schedule we'd have while here. I'd envisioned our stay as being laid back and relaxing. "You have a real Santa?"

"Oh, honey, Santa isn't real!" Aunt Paula burst into laughter, clapping with delight at her own joke. She could rival St. Nick in the jolly department.

I started to explain. "Well, I know. I meant—"

"Besides, Santa's not the real reason we do this. Christmas is about so much more than Santa!" Aunt Paula continued. "It's about Jesus and giving back and being with the ones you love."

"Right," I agreed, realizing I was taking myself entirely too seriously.

"We even have reindeer!" Aunt Paula's entire face beamed. She stuck a headband with antlers on my head and jingled the little bell on top with a delighted grin.

I glanced at Chad. *That's* what he wasn't telling me. I felt sure of it.

I cleared my throat. "Did you say reindeer? As in, *live* reindeer?"

She nodded, apparently clueless as to how I'd feel about that. There was too much excitement in her eyes for her to possibly know I was offended at the very notion.

"We raise them ourselves, right here on this property," she continued. "Chad didn't tell you that either?"

"No, he didn't," I said, my voice sickly sweet. My husband had kept this from me on purpose, which was curious. Why would he do that? He wasn't usually an avoid-conflict-at-all-costs type of guy.

I glanced over at him, but he didn't make eye contact.

"Now, I know you don't want to be bombarded. You just walked in. But we have got to get busy," Aunt Paula said, taking my arm. "So, let's put your suitcases down and get going, okay? We only have twenty-four hours until all the fun starts. Then we'll be jingle, jingle belling!"

She wiggled her hips like she was mentally listening—and dancing—to music.

I had no choice but to nod.

Instead, I operated on autopilot and followed Chad's aunt upstairs. I deposited my luggage in a rustic looking bedroom with reindeer embroidered on the burgundy coverlet before being ushered back downstairs.

"This is quite the house," I told his aunt. I'd arrived earlier than I intended, but everyone had been gone. I'd sat on the porch to wait for them, but this was my first glimpse of the home's interior.

She nodded. "Oh, I know. Isn't it grand? We just love it. How could you not?"

"And a reindeer farm? Here of all places? I had no idea." I gave Chad another look, but he turned away before he could catch it.

He knew exactly how I felt about farms and animals in captivity and the poor conditions most of them endured all in the name of "training." I also didn't approve of animals being used as entertainment or being handled like they were property.

"Now, let's give you a tour." His aunt grabbed something off the kitchen table and thrust it into my hands. "Here's some hot chocolate to get you started."

I started to object, but Chad shook his head. Apparently, his family didn't know I was a vegan and therefore didn't eat or drink any animal byproducts. I wondered if they even knew I was an animal rights activist.

Tension began to build between my shoulders. Chad had endured my crazy family, I reminded myself. I guess I needed to endure his now. And, I suppose that I hadn't told my family about our marriage, so I couldn't very well be mad at Chad for not telling his family the details of my life.

Unfortunately, this had the makings of a major disaster.

I held onto the hot chocolate as we stepped into the frigid outdoors. As soon as Aunt Paula looked away, I dumped the liquid into a bush. I didn't drink cow's milk, but I didn't want to offend her, so subtly ditching the liquid seemed like the best option.

We started toward the backyard. The ground felt hard and frozen beneath our feet, evidence of the especially cold winter. Part of me hoped it might snow while we were here because there was something about Christmas that beckoned a ground covered in white.

The backyard was huge with a large portion of the land cleared. Stables and a barn, along with a fenced in area, stood in the distance. There were tons of trees, most of them absent of any foliage, which made them look like skeletons standing guard over the property. The mountain was steep and the ground was covered with brown leaves.

Was this a reindeer farm?

I braced myself and tried to measure my reaction once I met the animals. After all, even someone like me—who was outspoken on all matters concerning animals—wanted to make a good impression on my in-laws. Tearing them apart or scolding them would not be a good idea—at all. Besides, I had more class than that, and I loved Chad too much.

"I guess Chad didn't tell you that our reindeer were even used in a movie once?" Aunt Paula asked, popping a peppermint into her mouth.

"A movie?" Animal treatment on the sets of movies was the worst. "No, he never told me that. Which one?"

"*Santa's Road Trip*. Do you remember that one?"

I nodded, vaguely recalling the name. I wondered if that's where Paul and Paula made their money. By all appearances, they weren't hurting for cash, not with a house this size on a piece of property this large. "I think I do."

"Yes, our reindeer are very special. They make Christmas feel like magic for kids. You'll see what we mean." She paused at a weathered wooden fence and looked around. "Now, I wonder where all my furry friends are?"

"Resting maybe?" I suggested.

She frowned. "As soon as they hear my voice, all my little darlings usually come running. They think it's feeding time. Their favorite is caramel popcorn, but we try not to give it to them. Every year at our light show, at least one unsuspecting visitor will have their bag snitched by one of the deer, though!"

And Chad hadn't even given me a hint about all of this. He'd only told me I was going to love it and that there was no one who loved Christmas more than his Aunt Paula and his Uncle Paul.

"Donner, Dasher, Prancer, Vixen!" Aunt Paula called.

Of *course* they'd be named that.

We waited but no one came.

No *reindeer* came, I should have said.

No reindeer who were being held captive here, outside of their native environment where, in the winter they were paraded around like Christmas royalty, all while being treated like four-legged slaves in the process. I'd seen it happen too many times before.

"Paul, go check around by the stables," Paula said. "Maybe they're all over there."

Paul nodded and started around the perimeter. He returned a few minutes later, his expression grim as he shook his head. "They're gone, Paula. All of them."

Paula sucked in a quick, loud breath. "What in heaven's name are you talking about? They can't be gone."

He nodded. "They are. And there are tire tracks proving someone backed right up to the gate and reindeer-napped them."

CHAPTER 2

"You think someone stole your reindeer?" Chad asked, gazing beyond her at the pasture as if the animals might magically appear. "Why would they do that?"

"Who knows?" Paula squeezed the skin between her eyes like she might cry. When she opened her eyes wide again, fire burned within their depths. "Maybe it's one of those crazy animal rights activists! They sent us some nasty notes not too long ago. I wouldn't put it past them. They threatened to take action against us!"

My cheeks reddened. Did *my* organization send Chad's relatives one of those letters? My coworkers were always on the lookout for the mistreatment of animals. We may even, on occasion, look for suitable campaigns that had a holiday tie in around Christmastime—but only because it made for better press opportunities. Getting the word out was half of the battle.

I wanted to slink back, but I couldn't.

Chad squeezed my hand.

"This is going to be awful. We can't have a Mountain Christmas Light Extravaganza without our reindeer!" Aunt Paula burst into tears, real ones this time, not the kind she tried to hide.

Paul pulled her toward him. "It's going to be okay. We'll find our beloved reindeer."

We began walking toward the gate. I had a feeling Paula wanted to see for herself that the reindeer were gone. I did too, for that matter.

"Do you think they could jump this fence?" I asked, shaking the sturdy structure.

Paul shook his head. "It's doubtful. They haven't ever done it before. None of them."

I leaned down by the tire tracks. There was a deep impression right by the gate, but otherwise the pattern faded quickly on the gravel. The ground was probably too frozen to leave many impressions.

"There are a few hoof prints right there," I said, pointing to the opening of the gate.

Paul nodded. "Then they disappear right here where a trailer would have pulled up."

I glanced beyond the driveway. The rest of the ground was blanketed with dry leaves. Finding any shoe impressions or hoof prints anywhere else seemed improbable.

"Should we call the sheriff?" Paula asked, her earlier jolly all gone.

Paul let out a loud sigh, his breath freezing in the frigid air. "I can't say Sheriff Orlando's going to jump right on this, given his dislike of our family. He'll come, but he'll drag his feet and claim he has speed traps to man or something asinine."

"That seems unethical," I said, outraged that someone could be that lackadaisical. It was the sheriff's job to help out in times like this.

Paula shook her head, popping another mint into her mouth. "Politics. That's what it is. We'll put in that phone call, but I don't expect him to take this seriously. What are we going to do?"

"Sierra's pretty good at tracking down answers. Aren't you, honey?" Chad said. "You remember when we were at your parents' house a couple of months ago and that dog—"

He stopped when he saw my narrowed eyes.

"Chad, can I talk to you?" I asked, batting my eyelashes sweetly—a sure signal something was wrong because I wasn't the bat-my-eyelids type of girl.

"Of course, dear." His words sounded stiff.

We walked far enough away that his aunt and uncle couldn't hear us. Still, I leaned close and lowered my voice. "Have you lost your mind?"

He stared at me contemplatively, as if trying to find the right words. "I want to say no, but I have a feeling I'm supposed to say yes . . . ."

"First of all, did you mention to your family that I am an animal rights activist?"

He cringed. "Not exactly."

"Why not?" My voice rose, and I mentally scolded myself. I had to keep my distress under wraps.

He rubbed his lips together for a moment, and I could see his inner turmoil. "I just didn't want them to form any impressions of you before they met you."

Surprise burst from me, unchecked. "What's that mean?"

He shushed me. "It means that you're great, but sometimes people hear 'animal rights activist,' and they think of crazy people."

"I'm not crazy—"

"*I* know that. But not everyone does. I wanted my family to meet you, fall in love with you, and then when they hear what you do for a living, it won't make a difference. We're in hunting, fishing, and farming country. Out here, animals are animals. It's a whole different world from yours."

"Thanks for the vote of confidence."

He rubbed my arms. "It *is* a vote of confidence.

You know how people have preconceived notions about things sometimes. Even you."

I gave him a skeptical glance.

"Admit it. You formed an immediate impression of my family as soon as you heard 'reindeer farm.' I'm just trying to play my cards right."

He had a point, but I didn't want to admit it. So, instead, I changed the subject. "And now you want me to track down the person who stole their reindeer. I applaud the person who took those poor creatures out of this environment. Hopefully the thieves took them somewhere they can thrive. Alaska or something!"

He leaned toward me, softening his voice. "What if they didn't? What if they took them somewhere to make venison jerky?"

I gasped so loud that his aunt and uncle turned to look at me. I forced a smile to reassure them before turning back to Chad. "That's an awful thing to say."

"Well, we have no idea where the reindeer are. They could be anywhere, even in the hands of someone . . . nefarious."

At once, I had the image of the Grinch, who then morphed into Scrooge. A meat eating Scrooge, at that. I knew I had to help. But something else was bugging me.

I narrowed my eyes, trying to process everything. "What are you really getting at here, Chad? Because I've never known you to actually encourage this behavior in me. You might go *along* with it. But never do you push me toward it."

His eyes softened. "I could help you."

I crossed my arms, sensing some ulterior motives lingering beneath the surface. "Why? Why do you want to help me?"

"Because I support you." He rubbed my arms again. "So, what do you say? Of course, I'd never want to do anything to put you in danger. If this turns ugly, you're out and I'm stringing lights. End of story. You're way more important than any reindeer."

I stared at him another moment, trying to read between the lines. "I've never seen this side of you."

He shrugged again. "What can I say? I'm an open minded kind of guy."

"We'll see about that." I nodded toward his family. "Let's go break the news."

I had to admit that looking for the reindeer-nappers seemed more appealing than sitting in a house with that stuffed reindeer head staring back at me.

We made our way back toward Paul and Paula.

"Chad and I would like to help you find the reindeer," I started. "If you'd like our help, of course."

Paula clapped and let out a long sigh. "Oh, we'd love that, Sierra. Chad said you were an angel. It sounds like he was right."

***

I got the basic information I needed from Paul and Paula. There were twelve reindeer. The last time anyone had seen them was this morning at ten a.m. when Paul went out to feed them. It was now one p.m., so they'd disappeared sometime between then and now. Everyone in town knew about the reindeer and came out in droves at Christmastime to see them. The only people Paul and Paula could possibly think of who didn't like the reindeer were their neighbors, the Nimbles. They complained to the county every year at Christmas because of the increased traffic on the normally placid mountain road.

With that said, Chad and I decided to go into town to begin our search and rescue mission. Coincidentally, we also had to pick up some additional extension cords at the hardware store for the light show. I supposed that it was good for

Paula to keep her mind occupied with mundane details instead of fretting.

We headed down the road in Chad's Vanagon. Yes, *his* Vanagon. We might be married, but it would always be his vehicle, not mine.

I glanced over at my husband as he drove, seeing a new side of him now that we were here in his hometown. He'd grown a beard for no-shave November and decided to keep it. He looked a bit like a rugged mountain man instead of a sun-kissed surfer dude. He'd topped his head with a knit hat, wore a flannel jacket, jeans, and work boots, and smelled like the woods.

In other words, I'd married a lumberjack.

Other than that fact, I thought he was extremely handsome, as well as kind, caring, and hardworking.

"So, you want to tell me the real reason why you're volunteering to help me out now? I've never seen you so eager," I started.

"Eager? That's putting it strongly."

"No, it's not. You seem a little *too* anxious to help me. Are you desperately trying to get out of putting up Christmas lights?"

He remained stoic a moment before saying, "It's like this. I know you're going to get involved, Sierra. I had no doubt in my mind when I heard animals were involved and possibly in peril that you'd want to help. I can't send you out there alone."

"Send me out there alone?" I repeated, feeling like there was some kind of war going on that I didn't know about.

He nodded. "I've got to look out for you, especially now that you're having a baby. There's no way I'm going to let you get in trouble without being by your side to help in case something goes wrong."

I wanted to argue, but deep inside, I thought it was sweet. He'd been doting over me ever since he found out we were expecting a couple of months ago. As long as he didn't make me feel suffocated, I'd let him do his thing.

We wound down the mountain road and a small town came into sight. "This is right out of a painting," I said, peering out the window in awe.

And it was. Main Street was perfect, filled with old timey buildings—most of them three or four stories high—and a quaint streetscape. Candy canes were on the light posts and a lovely view of the mountains surrounded the area. The gray sky seemed to promise that snow could be on the way.

"Nice, isn't it?" he asked, pulling into a space in front of a drug store.

"It reminds me of Mayberry."

"Mayberry? Nah. Oldsburgh is better than Mayberry."

"I'm surprised you ever left this place if it's so great." Chad had lived here before moving to Virginia. Before that he'd been a mortician in Kansas. His dad was military, so his family had moved around quite a bit.

"There's not much to do in terms of crime scene cleaning here in Oldsburgh. Plus, it's really hard to surf around here."

"What *do* people do around here?"

"They either work here in town, at the factory down by the river, or at the ski resort just up the mountain. Some people drive to the next town over for work. It's about forty-five minutes away."

"I see." This was a totally different kind of life than where I'd grown up or even where I lived now. I'd never been a small town girl and definitely not a small town *mountain* girl. The idea had its appeal, however. Except for the hunting, fishing, and farming aspects.

"I say we start in the coffee shop," Chad said. "What do you say? Maybe we can grab a hot cup of java in the meantime."

I nodded. "Sounds great to me. Hopefully the coffee is free trade."

"My thoughts exactly."

He raised his eyebrows comically, and I knew those *weren't* his thoughts exactly. I was picky, so I didn't expect everyone to understand my convictions. I was just happy to have found someone who let me be who I was. That was a rare commodity.

It was time to find out what everyone had seen, rescue those reindeer, and . . . then what? Place the poor creatures back into captivity?

I wasn't sure, but I needed to figure out something soon.

Certainly there was a win-win in here somewhere, for me and the reindeer.

CHAPTER 3

We asked around at several stores in town and even stopped several people we met on the sidewalk. However, no one had seen a trailer loaded with reindeer dashing through the snow today. I mean, really, how did someone take off down the road with twelve reindeer and no witnesses?

At the hardware store, while picking up those extension cords, I had another idea. Vernon, the owner, had apparently lived here forever and knew everyone. The older man looked so bent over that he could barely stand, yet I had a feeling he'd work at this store until the day he died. He was the perfect person to talk to.

"Do you know anyone in town who has a trailer big enough to hold twelve reindeer?" I leaned on the nicked up counter of the store, inhaling the faint scent of motor oil and sawdust.

Vernon paused, as did Chad and the two other employees who'd joined the conversation.

Probably because it was such a genius question that everyone was wondering why they hadn't thought of it first.

Then chuckles emerged from the crowd. The sound grew in propensity until everyone was downright laughing. Except for Chad, who quickly sobered when he looked at the angled eyebrows of my scowl.

"Around here everyone has trailers," Vernon said. "They use them for horses or cattle or sheep going to auction."

I frowned and, for no good reason, gave Chad a dirty look like all of this was his fault.

My dear husband cleared his throat and straightened as if he was a kid with his hand caught in the cookie jar. "Unless you've lived in a place like this, it's hard to comprehend what everyday life is like. And with that said, we should be going."

"Chad, before you go, I need to order something from your uncle," Vernon started. "Do you think—?"

"You should probably call him yourself," Chad said, pulling me toward the door. "Believe me, I'll forget before I get back. All I can think about are reindeer and Christmas lights."

Vernon smiled. "It's that time of year. I'll call him."

Well, that was a strange exchange. I shook my head, marking it up to some kind of close-knit community dynamic that I'd probably never understand. Apparently, there was a lot about living here that I'd never understand.

As we started down the street, I looped my arm through Chad's. "If I'm understanding all of this correctly, we just narrowed our suspect list down to nearly everyone in town. What's that? A thousand people?"

"It was a good try. Now, if you'd asked that question in Norfolk, you really could narrow it down. Out here in mountain country, trailers are as common as toilet paper. People use them for a lot of things."

I paused by a bench, pushing aside the feeling that I'd been sucked into a Lifetime holiday movie. Even worse, something about this warm, cozy town made me want to go Christmas shopping . . . and caroling . . . and light a Christmas tree in the town square, which, by the way, even had a gazebo. This place was toying with all of my pent up Christmas fantasies.

Focus, Sierra. Focus.

Where did I go to look for stolen reindeer next?

I remembered the letters that may have been sent to Paul and Paula from an animal rights group.

Maybe I could find some leads there. At the least, maybe I could alleviate my anxiety that someone I knew had sent the correspondence.

"You know what, I need to call my office," I told Chad, moving out of the way as some Christmas shoppers scurried past with bags in hand. "I want to make sure Paws and Furballs never sent any of those nasty grams to your family. If they did, I should just leave town now."

"You don't mean that."

"What will your family think when they find out the truth about me?"

He shrugged, pulling his collar up as a brisk wind swept over the sidewalk. "They're pretty easy going."

"Did you hear their voices when they talked about animal rights activists?" I couldn't get the exchange out of my head. Paula had sounded absolutely disgusted with the person who'd sent it.

"Maybe . . . ."

I shook my head. "I don't want to talk about it. I just want to call and either ease or confirm my fears."

I pulled out my phone and dialed my office. My assistant answered. "Cindy, it's Sierra reporting in from Mayberry."

"Mayberry?"

I crossed my free arm across my stomach and leaned against the store behind me. It was a toy shop boasting a train and Christmas village in its picture window. "Or you could call it the world's happiest town where Christmas saturates every fiber of its being. Seriously. Its citizens, its buildings, and probably even its air traffic control flight pattern are consumed with this holiday at this time of year."

"Sounds nice. Just like the kind of place I'd like to be."

Something deep inside me wanted to argue, but I couldn't. This place was pretty perfect.

"Either way, I have a question. Has anyone from Paws and Furballs ever started a campaign against something called Mountain Christmas Light Magic?"

"It doesn't sound familiar to me."

"Me either, but that doesn't mean that someone from the organization didn't take initiative to send them a letter. The, uh . . . organizers . . . have reindeer that are used at Christmas activities in the areas."

"They sound despicable, using those poor animals to promote their own agendas."

I remembered Paula and Paul's smiling faces. My intuitive agreement dissipated. "Not despicable. But it's important that I know if there's anything there."

"One second," Cindy said. Computer keys tapped in the background.

"Merry Christmas!" A woman with rosy cheeks stuffed something into my hand as she passed. She wore an old timey dress, complete with a bonnet and cape, and carried a basket full of treats, courtesy of the town of Oldsburgh, if I had to guess.

I saw that she'd given me a candy cane. Maybe the peppermint would calm down my stomach some. It hadn't been right since I found out I was pregnant.

"Nothing's coming up through my computer search. I can ask around, though, just to be sure someone wasn't acting as a lone ranger," Cindy said.

"That would be great. I need to know ASAP. And let's keep this quiet, okay? I don't want anyone at Paws and Furballs to know I'm connected with it. Not now, at least."

"Oh, sounds mysterious. I'll call you back today."

I joined Chad on the sidewalk. Every time the wind blew, it cut all the way through to my bones, even though I wore a puffy red vest and turtleneck.

My nose even felt frozen; I only hoped it didn't look as red as Rudolph's.

I gave Chad the update.

"So what now?" I asked, glancing around.

The same woman who'd given me the candy cane now stood on the corner, belting out "Silver Bells" in a high soprano. Other people shopped or chatted with friends while strolling through town. A couple people browsed the Christmas tree stand on the corner. However, there were no reindeer to be seen.

"Good question," Chad said.

"So far, we've not only narrowed the culprit down to nearly the whole town, but it seems like everyone loves your family and their light show. So, everyone has means but no one has motive."

"Except their neighbors," Chad added.

That was right. The neighbors hated the Christmas light show. We definitely needed to talk to them. Since I had no other good ideas, they were the logical ones to approach next.

Just then, a little boy who looked like he was around six years old, walked up to me and tugged at my vest. He had dark hair and brown eyes. Instantly, I had visions of my own child. What would he or she look like? Maybe he'd have Chad's sandy colored hair. Or would she have my dark hair

and Asian features? Would the child be laidback
like Chad or zealous like me?

Warm fuzzies filled me at the thought. Life at
this time next year would be very different than life
right now.

"Can I help you?" I asked the boy. I glanced
around. Where was the boy's mom? Even in
Oldsburgh, it seemed like a good idea to have a
parent or guardian around.

The boy pointed at me. "I love hot hookers."

My mouth dropped open. I looked down at
myself. Nothing about the jeans and sensible
clothes I wore screamed prostitute. Who was this
boy? He no longer seemed quite as cute and
innocent.

He pointed to my hands and licked his lips. "Hot
hookers."

I held up the card I'd been given on the
sidewalk, beginning to piece things together. "You
mean, candy canes?"

He frowned. "They're hot and hooked. And I
can never remember . . . what are they called
again?"

"Candy canes," I told him.

"Right, candy canes. Do you want that,
ma'am?"

I handed my peppermint treat to him. "It's all

yours."

I glanced at Chad and saw a smile tugging at his lips. "Interesting terminology, kid."

He turned to Chad, his eyes widening. "And you—are you Santa's son?"

Chad's smile disappeared and his shoulders visibly tightened. "What was that?"

The boy pointed to Chad's beard, his high-pitched voice and slight lips making him hard to get angry with. "If your beard was white, you'd look just like Santa."

"Except I'm thinner," Chad said slowly, offense creeping into his voice. "Right?"

Chad had gained about ten pounds since we'd been married, and he was feeling self-conscious. So far this kid had managed to insult both of us. It was quite a talent he had.

"If you say so, Mister." The boy stepped closer, his face turning serious. "Listen, can you give Santa a message from me? There's something I really want to talk to him about."

Chad squatted down. "Maybe I can. Or you could go talk to Santa yourself at the light show tomorrow night."

The boy's eyes lit. "I love that show! It's my favorite."

"Are you coming this year?" I continued,

determined to prove I was good with kids. I had my doubts. Make that *fears*. What if I wasn't a good mother? And how would I ever really know that for sure until I *became* a mother? By then, my child would be stuck with me, and I'd ruin him or her for life.

He nodded. "I wouldn't miss it! Okay, I've gotta go meet my parents. Bye Santa's son and hot hooker lady."

I glanced at Chad. This was going to be a fun trip.

Or not.

CHAPTER 4

"What now?" Chad asked, tucking in his stomach. He was still thin, his face just looked more filled out. But he was nowhere close to looking like Santa.

"Now you take some deep breaths and remember that those remarks came from an innocent, naïve child who didn't know better."

"Okay, hot hooker lady." He grinned.

I elbowed him. "Anyway, I say we pay a visit to the neighbors. You said the reindeer are one of the highlights of the show, right? Maybe the Nimbles are hoping that without the reindeer, the show won't go on."

"Maybe. I guess it's a theory." He shook his head. "The missing reindeer could devastate my aunt and uncle. They look forward to this all year. You should see it, Sierra. They have cookies and hot chocolate. They have live music, a live Santa, and the reindeer. People come from all over the state. They can only do it for the three days leading up to

Christmas, though. It's just too much of a cash drain to do it for any longer."

"You mean, they don't charge?" I shoved my hands into my pockets as we started toward the Vanagon.

He shook his head. "They consider this their Christmas gift to the community."

"That's awfully generous of them."

"That's what kind of people they are."

I nodded, fully aware that a lot of good people didn't share my exact viewpoints.

"It's just too bad your parents aren't here," I said.

"Yeah, I agree," he said. "But I know they're having fun on their cruise. They work hard, so it's good for them to get away. The Caribbean does sound awfully nice, doesn't it?"

Before I climbed into the van, something on the ground caught my eye. I reached down and picked it up. It was a bell, probably an inch and a half wide, with a red ribbon around it. The ends of the ribbon looked frayed, as if it had broken off from something, and the material itself was dirty and old.

Strange. I couldn't just throw it back on the ground, so I stuffed it into my pocket and climbed into the van.

Just as I slammed the door, a man in a sheriff's uniform paused on the street corner. He stared right at Chad and I, his eyes narrowing.

"Is that *the* sheriff?" I asked Chad.

Chad peered through the window. "Yep, that's him. Sheriff Orlando."

"Sounds like there's bad blood between him and your family." I snapped on my seatbelt.

"Yeah, you could say that. That man knows how to hold onto a grudge."

"What happened?"

"Rumor has it that my Uncle Paul moved to town and swept Paula off her feet. Apparently, the sheriff had his eye on her, and he still feels like Paul 'stole' his woman. Ridiculous, huh?"

Interesting.

Ten minutes later, after we traveled away from town and back into the heart of the mountains, I pointed to a road with a sign reading "Collards 4 Sale." It was the driveway before Paul and Paula's. I'd seen it on my way into town.

He nodded toward the crooked black mailbox beside the crude-looking sign. "Says the 'Nimbles.' Must be the place."

We pulled down the narrow, rocky lane, one that was filled with potholes and steep inclines. It had to be difficult to travel this when it snowed. A small, dumpy house stood at the end of the lane.

It was white clapboard with a small cement porch and clothes strung on the lines between the porch posts. The house itself couldn't have more than four or five rooms. Junk was strewn around the perimeter, including tires, rocking chairs, and an old tractor.

I didn't want to stereotype, but this seemed like the house of someone who was backward, who'd removed themselves from society and its expectations.

There was an old barn behind the house, but half of it had collapsed. There was also some kind of grain elevator that looked like it hadn't been used in years.

I half expected someone with a shotgun to walk onto the porch and demand we tell him why we were here. Unfortunately, in my mind this person was wearing overalls and had a beard similar to Chad's. Yep, I was pretty much picturing the Clampetts.

That didn't happen, though. In fact, we knocked at the door but no one answered.

So much for finding some answers.

I had to admit that someone who had this much trouble managing their yard and their house might have trouble managing to steal a bunch of reindeer without anyone noticing. That didn't mean they were off my suspect list, though.

As we climbed back into the van, my cell phone rang. It was Cindy.

"Sierra, I've checked with everyone in the office, and no one said they've sent anything to this reindeer farm you mentioned. However, I did find it interesting that Good Day Fishing Hooks are also manufactured there in Oldsburgh. We have talked about sending them correspondence in the past, though I have no record we've done anything yet."

"Really?" I wondered if that was the factory that Chad had mentioned, the one that employed most of the people in town. "I'm not sure that has anything to do with the reindeer, however."

"You want me to draft a letter to them? Maybe you'll have more influence now that you're married to someone who has family in the area."

I considered it a moment. "Go ahead and draft up something. But don't send it without my approval."

"Got it."

"Can you do me one more favor? Can you check to see if there's anyone in our network of supporters who lives anywhere near Oldsburgh, West Virginia?"

"Sure thing. I can do that now if you can wait

just a minute."

I motioned for Chad to stay put.

"Let's see. I narrowed it down to West Virginia, now I'm searching through the cities." Cindy clucked her tongue. "What do you know? We do have one supporter who lives right in Oldsburgh. His name is Sam Bills. Would you like his address?"

"Would I ever." I grabbed an old napkin from the floor and a pen from my purse and jotted it down.

I knew exactly where we needed to head next.

***

Sam Bills lived about twenty minutes away on a narrow mountain road that was lined with houses. A small stream trickled behind the homes to my left. Most of the houses were smaller in size and also had clapboard siding, just like the Nimbles. However, some were not well-kept, while others had neat grass and nicely shaped flowerbeds. This area and the diversity here fascinated me. I'd lived in the city. I'd lived in suburbia. But I'd never lived anywhere like this.

We pulled up to a house that had yellow siding and an economy-sized car parked in the driveway. The car had a Paws and Furballs bumper sticker on the back.

This had to be the right place.

"Do you know this Sam Bills?" I asked Chad, chomping at the bit to talk to the man . . . er, I meant feeling *anxious* to talk to him. Bits in the mouths of horses were inhumane, whether in reality or when used as an expression.

He shook his head. "He must have moved here after I left."

"Let me do the talking then," I told Chad, stepping from the Vanagon.

I climbed the steps, knocked on the door, and straightened my shirt as I waited for someone to answer. A moment later, a man who was about my age pulled the door open. He had thinning blonde hair, pale skin, and a slouched stance that only emphasized the solitary collection of weight in his stomach. The scent of . . . was that bacon? . . . drifted from the interior.

The man stared at me a moment.

Before I could introduce myself, his face lit up like a . . . uh, well, a Christmas tree.

"Sierra Nakamura—I mean, Davis?" he said.

I put my hand down, taken back and thrown off guard. "Do I know you?"

He shook his head, and I immediately saw it.

I saw the crazy in his eyes and braced myself for

whatever happened next.

CHAPTER 5

Sam Bills opened the screen door and stepped closer—a little too close. "You're one of my idols."

I pointed to myself as I scooted back. Chad grasped my elbow as my foot caught the edge of the porch. Thank goodness he was here. "I'm one of your idols?"

He nodded. "That's right. I love Paws and Furballs. I follow almost everything you guys do. You all blow my mind."

"I'm . . . I'm flattered," I told him.

"What are you doing here? Did you come to . . . to recruit me? Oh my goodness. Is this the call? *The* call? Are there cameras around?" He craned his neck to peek behind me. "Because this would make a great feel good holiday video. You're making my dreams come true! Of *course* I'll work for you!"

I shook my head, trying to cut that thought off quickly before he ran with it. "No, I'm sorry. I wish I could say that. But I have something you could help me with."

His smile turned into a frown and then the next second his hopeful expression returned. "Anything. I'm on it. Is it about the fishermen out here? I've never been a big fan of the sport myself. It's not as bad as crabbing, though. Did you know that people boil crabs alive—?"

"It's not about fishing, Sam. Or crabbing," I told him. I stole a glance at Chad. He looked thoroughly entertained.

"Then it's about hunting? People hunt around here like some people watch TV. They live for it. I don't care what anyone says about controlling the animal population—"

I shook my head. "That's not it either."

"That recent oil spill up north that affected the river and killed wildlife?"

I shook my head again, fascinated by everything he was saying but trying to stay focused. "I'm sorry, Sam. It's actually about the reindeer farm here in town."

His lips parted. "Oh, the reindeer farm. Over at the Davis' place? Of course. What about it?"

I tried to think of a less in-your-face way to approach this. The man did seem over-the-top. I didn't want his emotions to spike to the other side, plunging into the depths of anger instead of excitement. "Do you know of anyone who'd want to free those reindeer?"

"Free the reindeer? Were they not being treated well? I should have known. That Paul Davis, he may be a nice man, but he's always talking about hunting. He *loves* killing animals for his own enjoyment. How can someone who loves to *eat* deer have *pet* deer? Because that's essentially what reindeer are."

I reached behind me and squeezed Chad's arm, hoping he wasn't offended. Knowing Chad, Mr. Laidback himself, he was simply enjoying this. Crazy people were immensely entertaining. That's what he'd told me once. "Anyone else around here share your sentiments?"

He looked toward the sky and sighed. "I don't know. Probably."

"Do you know anyone who would steal them?" I asked. I had a feeling this man didn't have the gumption to do it himself.

"Steal them?" He snorted.

When he saw my face, he turned serious again.

"I mean, I guess someone might want to steal them. But exactly how would they do that? Wouldn't they need a sleigh or something?" He snorted again as if this was some kind of bad Christmas joke.

He must have noticed that I didn't appreciate his humor, because his laugh abruptly stopped. "I mean, no, I really don't know of anyone in particular who would steal the reindeer."

I stepped closer, narrowing my eyes like a prosecutor about to do a killer cross-examination. "How about you? Would you do it?"

His eyes widened, and he stepped back, nearly tripping over the door jamb.

Was that a look of guilt in his eyes?

Maybe I'd underestimated the man.

"You've got to believe me. I'm an all talk kind of guy," he insisted, panic fluttering in his gaze and shaking his voice.

I crossed my arms. "What does that mean?"

"It just means that I like to talk a lot, to say a lot without really saying anything. But I very rarely put any action behind my words. Call it hypocritical, but that's what I do." His words came out fast, rushed.

"So, you've made threats. Is that what I'm understanding?"

"I . . . may have sent the family a couple of letters."

"Really?"

He cringed. "And I may have lain like a dead fish outside of Good Day Fishing Hooks with a sign saying, 'Fish Have Feelings Too.'"

"You didn't claim to be with Paws and Furballs, did you?"

He shrugged again. "Maybe I did throw it in there. I do support the organization."

"That doesn't give you a right to use their name, you know." I felt like a mom scolding a toddler, which only renewed my parental fears, especially when I saw Sam's bottom lip droop with remorse.

"I know. I just wanted to make a difference. It's my dream to work for you guys."

"What do you do?" Something about the man didn't sit right with me.

"I'm a . . ." He tugged at his collar. "A driver."

"For what company?"

He cringed, suddenly sweating. "For one of the logging companies the next town over."

"So you want to save the animals but ruin the environment?" It was hypocrisy at its finest.

"A man can only have so many passions."

I rolled my eyes. "But you did have access to some large trucks. Trucks that may hold reindeer."

He ran a hand through his thin hair, causing a wisp of it to stand on end. "I didn't steal any reindeer. Like I said, I talk the talk but don't walk the walk. I eat meat, for goodness sakes! Check my freezer."

I didn't have to. I definitely smelled bacon in the background. It was an unmistakable scent. If I wasn't a vegan, I might even call it mouthwatering.

I stared at the man, unable to believe my ears. I wanted to tell him that he made animal lovers look bad, but I bit my tongue.

"Mr. Bills, where were you between 10 a.m. and 1 p.m. today?"

"I was at the hardware store in town all morning, trying to get something to fix my washing machine. I just got home about two hours ago. Ask anyone. They'll confirm it."

"I think I'll do that." With that, I turned on my heel and stomped back to the van.

"Can I have your autograph?" Sam yelled behind me, obviously not dissuaded by my disgruntled scowl.

I didn't say anything, just climbed into the van and locked the door behind me.

"You're like a celebrity in the animal rights world, aren't you?" Chad said, cranking the engine. Blissfully warm air flooded through the vents.

"No, I'm not a celebrity. But I do lead a great group of people. It's quite possibly the best job ever."

"Happy wife, happy life. That's what my dad

always taught me."

"But a woman is only as happy as her man." I reached over and kissed his furry cheek. "Funny the way that works, isn't it?"

"Beautiful, actually." He squeezed my hand before pulling onto the road. "So, what do you want to do now?"

I leaned back, trying to think clearly. Chad's family had high hopes that we would find some answers, and I hated to disappoint them. But, as the sun began to set, my options were becoming limited.

"It's getting dark. I'm not sure how much more we can do tonight," I started. "What do you say we get back and see if your aunt and uncle have heard anything?"

"Sounds like a plan."

We cruised along for several minutes in silence, the only sound was that of the Beach Boys singing Christmas classics. The road was winding and thick with trees on either side of it.

Chad cleared his throat and glanced over at me. "Look, before we go back, there's something I should probably tell you."

I wrinkled my forehead, eyebrows drawn together. "Okay."

"It's about my uncle. He—"

Before Chad had a chance to finish his sentence, a deer appeared in the middle of the road.

Or was it a . . . reindeer?

I didn't have time to contemplate.

Chad slammed on the brakes.

I prepared myself for the worst.

CHAPTER 6

As if in slow motion, the van skidded.

Rubber burned.

Tires screeched.

The deer froze, his gaze piercing us.

My hands went to the dashboard, waiting for impact.

My future flashed before my eyes.

Specifically, the future of my dear, sweet baby.

What if something happened to my unborn child? I couldn't stand the thought of it. My heart clutched with grief at the notion.

Oh God, please help!

Finally, the van stopped.

My heart pounded into my rib cage as I tried to absorb what had happened.

Had we hit the deer? Was anyone hurt? Chad? Me?

Bambi still stood there, staring at us. He blinked once and then darted back into the woods as if this was a game and he'd just scored a point.

"Are you okay?" Chad asked, worry lacing his eyes.

I nodded, feeling numb and shaky. "Yeah, I think so. We're . . . we're okay. Right?"

"Are you sure you're okay?" Chad asked. His gaze went to my stomach. "And the baby. Is the baby okay? I'm taking you to the hospital. That's all there is to it."

"Really, I'm fine."

"What about the baby?"

"I'm just shaken, Chad. If I start feeling bad, I'll let you know. I promise."

He stared at me another moment, and I wondered if he'd take off toward the hospital despite my protests. "These reindeer games are starting to get to me. We're going back home for the night, and you're taking it easy. I insist."

I nodded, not in the mood to argue. "It's a plan."

***

Everyone was still busy stringing Christmas lights as we pulled up to the house. This certainly would be a winter wonderland. I was still trembling from our near accident, and I wasn't going to argue with Chad about staying put for the rest of the

CHRISTY BARRITT

night. I needed my heart to slow down some.

"Chad! Sierra! You're back," Paula said, meeting us at the van. "You're just in time for the magic."

"The magic?" I questioned, stuffing my hands into my pockets before she noticed them trembling.

She grinned. "That's right. We're doing our light test."

"I can't believe you have time to put this up just a few days before Christmas." Everywhere I looked there were cords and strings of lights and lawn ornaments and everything else you could possibly think of pertaining to Christmas. It was quite the undertaking.

"Oh, don't be silly. A lot of it we leave up all year. But there are a few things we have to put up at the last minute. Otherwise, the sun and wind would ruin it. Still, it's a huge task—at times an overwhelming one. But it's worth it to see the smiles on the children's faces."

"You ready, Paula?" Uncle Paul yelled from around the side of the house.

"Ready, Paul!" she hollered over her shoulder.

Just then, the lights came on. I let out a little gasp as white pinprick-sized bulbs sprinkled the trees above me. Christmas music—"White Christmas," to be specific—crooned through the

62

overhead speakers. Animatronic bears began ice skating on a fake pond within spitting distance.

"You're right. This is magical," I whispered, my neck craned back so I could get a better view.

Paula grinned. "See, I told you. We're not even done yet. Now, let's go inside for a minute. I bet you guys haven't had anything to eat and that's simply unacceptable."

I could only imagine what dinner might hold. My gut feeling was a lot of meat. And cheese. Maybe even warm milk and cookies made with eggs.

I didn't want to be impolite. I really didn't. But I didn't know how I would gracefully get out of this one. Of course, I'd brought nuts with me and some apples. Pulling those out during dinner wouldn't help my likability factor, though.

We sat down, and Grandma ladled out some beef vegetable soup. The savory scent made my stomach grumble. I could eat around the beef, I decided. It was the lesser of the evils around me— both morally and socially.

After we prayed, we dug in. Unfortunately, Chad and I were the only ones eating, which meant Grandma and Aunt Paula had the opportunity to watch our every move—or should I say, our every bite?

As I sipped on the warm, salty broth, my gaze kept going toward the reindeer head hanging on the wall in the living room, which was within eyesight of where I sat at the table. How could someone who proclaimed to love reindeer so much stuff one and use him as a decoration? It made no sense to me.

"You looking at St. Nick over there?" Paula asked, following my gaze.

I felt my cheeks heat as I nodded. I only hoped my thoughts hadn't been transparent. "I am."

Paula pressed her lips together, suddenly looking somber. "He was a great reindeer. Our first. He was so good with the kids. When he died, I couldn't imagine just burying him, so we had him stuffed. This way, it's like he's always here with us."

"So, it's a little . . . memorial to him, I guess."

Paula nodded and set a basket of freshly baked rolls from the oven in the middle of the table. My mouth watered. They looked and smelled so tasty. Something about this pregnancy was making me not want to be a vegan anymore. I could only imagine the reactions of people at my work if they found out I'd started eating animals, though. They'd never let me live it down. They may even lynch me, right before telling me to look for a new job.

No one liked a hypocrite.

"As soon as we finish up, I thought maybe we could have a fire. Marshmallows, anyone?" Grandma said. "It will be just like old times."

Marshmallows? They sounded wonderful, especially toasted over an open fire.

But marshmallows were made of gelatin, and gelatin was made from boiling the bones of cows and pigs. In other words, the sweet treat was off limits. Sometimes convictions required sacrifice.

Sometimes, if I were totally honest, I resented the sacrifice.

"We can have fun all we want tonight, Grandma." Aunt Paula frowned. "But I won't have any peace, not until my precious reindeer are back here."

CHAPTER 7

That night, after everyone had finished working, eaten dinner, and nibbled on Christmas sweets, we all gathered around the fireplace. Uncle Paul pulled out his guitar and we sang Christmas carols like "Chestnuts Roasting on an Open Fire" and "Silent Night." A couple of people from town who were "practically family" joined us. I'd realized after only being here a short time that half the people in town were "practically family" to the Davises. I thought that inclusion was a good quality to have, though. Refreshing, really.

As Uncle Paul sang in a rich tenor, the mellow sound of the acoustic guitar soothed me. I couldn't sing worth a lick, but I moved my lips, wishing I could carry a tune. Occasionally, a few lyrics escaped from me, almost as if Christmas spirit was a happy, joy-filled virus that spread through the house. Chad tucked his arm around me and endorphins warmed my heart.

This was going to be a perfect Christmas.

"You're glowing, you know," Grandma said when Uncle Paul put away the guitar and the conversations around us turned smaller and more intimate. "I can already tell that motherhood is going to suit you."

"I hope so." I realized too late that I'd said the words aloud, and I gulped, hoping she wouldn't judge me.

"Oh, Sierra, my dear. Every new mother has those kinds of fears. The fact that you're worried about it is usually a signal that you're going to be a great mother. Worrying shows you care."

I smiled, her words bringing a wave of peace over me. "Thanks, Grandma."

Her bony, wrinkled hand squeezed mine. "I'm just so thrilled to see that Chad is so happy. That says a lot about you, Sierra. I knew it would take someone really special to capture his heart."

Before I could get choked up—which I was well on my way to doing—Paula sat on the other side of me and thrust a fresh mug of hot chocolate in my hands. I really needed to let her know I was a vegan, but the words just wouldn't leave my lips. It was strange, because I usually proclaimed my viewpoints from the mountaintops. Was I losing my passion? Or was I just growing up and learning to be more temperate?

"Christmas is all about family," Paula said with a content smile. "Isn't this just wonderful? We're here, celebrating each other and celebrating the birth of Christ. It doesn't get any better."

"I have to agree."

Her smile slipped. "The only thing that makes my heart heavy is my poor reindeer. I just can't believe they're gone. I have to stop myself from thinking worst-case scenarios. It messed with my Christmas mojo."

"How long have the reindeer been a part of your life?"

She stared into the fire. "For the last seven years. Animal control found them abandoned in the next county. Someone was trying to raise them, but ran out of money and left everything behind. We adopted them. We had the space here—plenty of wide open fields and shelter. They've been a joy to us."

"So, you rescued them?" I stated, my heart softening.

Perhaps I'd too quickly judged. It wouldn't be the first time—or the last, unfortunately.

"In a way, they rescued us," Aunt Paula continued. "They've given us something to look forward to. When we adopted them, our oldest daughter had just moved out, and Paul and I were feeling the strain of empty nest. Those little darlings gave us new life." She laughed and shook her head, her gaze connecting with mine. "I sound crazy, don't I?"

"No, you don't. Animals have a way of cheering people up. We can bond with them in ways that are unexpected." I knew that better than anyone. Cats had been my sanity while growing up with two parents who worked too much. My feline friends had been the ones who'd accepted me without judgment, something I'd desperately needed.

"Yes, it's true. I sure do hope they're okay. The only thing that's stopping me from going crazy is thinking about the joy of the children when they see the lights here. I have to go on with this Light Extravaganza for their sake."

"I think it's really great what you do for the community," I told her.

"I really think I get so much out of other people's joy that I'm the one being a little selfish." She laughed at herself again before standing. "Anyway, we're going to go make some pies. It's the only thing we sell during the show, but we do it for a good cause. We always give the money to a needy family in the area."

I hesitated briefly, visions of butter and milk and eggs dancing in my head. I did have a great recipe for my specialty acorn brownies, one that required none of those animal byproducts. However, I didn't think anyone would go for the idea.

Finally, I decided to roll with it. "That sounds great, Paula."

It wasn't until I got in bed later that night that I realized Chad had started to tell me something earlier, right before we'd seen the deer in the road and nearly crashed.

I wondered what it was. As he let out a snore beside me, I sighed.

I guessed I'd find out soon enough. But I wouldn't wake him from his slumber now.

***

The next morning, I felt a renewed sense of purpose. The light show started tonight, and I desperately wanted to find the reindeer for Paul and Paula. It was important to them, so for that reason, it was important to me, also. Plus, I didn't like wondering where the poor creatures were and if they were okay. They deserved to be safe and cared for.

Last night had solidified my resolve. Being with Chad's relatives made me feel like I was a part of something, something greater than my animal rights organization even. It made me feel like I was a part of a loving family. I hadn't realized how much I desired that acceptance until now.

Professionally speaking, I was outspoken and nervy. But relationally, I was private and often reserved. It took a lot for me to let people get beyond my walls and see the real me. I found myself wanting that unconditional love of family now. Maybe it was the baby. Maybe it was the fact that my own family was just now on the mend after years of tension. I wasn't sure.

Whatever the reason, right after breakfast, Chad and I went to pay a visit to the Nimbles again. This time, there was an old truck parked in the driveway. I took that as a good sign and hoped for the best. Maybe we'd finally find some answers.

As we knocked at the door and waited, an odd smell drifted out from inside the home.

"What is that?" I whispered to Chad, not certain if I should turn my nose up or pull out a fork.

"Greens," Chad said.

"Greens?"

"You know, collard greens."

I'd tried a lot of vegetables in my life, but never collards. "They smell . . . awful."

"They actually taste pretty good, especially with some pepper vinegar and raw onions on top."

Just then, a woman pulled the door open. She looked like she'd seen better days. Dark circles hung underneath her eyes, her hair looked like it hadn't been combed, and her clothing was stained and ill-fitted. I wasn't a hugger, but instantly wanted to pull the woman into my arms and tell her everything would be okay.

"Can I help you?" She kept one hand on the door like she might slam it at any minute.

Chad looked at me, leaving the ball in my court. I told him earlier that I would handle this. He was always great for back up though, for when my mouth or my opinions got me in trouble. I loved it that he let me be myself, even in uncomfortable situations.

Such as this one.

"Hi, I'm Sierra and I'm staying next door with the Davis family. It seems their reindeer have gone missing, and we wondered if you knew anything about it. Since you live so close, we thought maybe you'd seen something."

She blinked several times before speaking, her voice absent of emotion. "You think I stole some reindeer?"

I shifted. I'd thought my words had been

especially careful and non-judgmental. "I didn't say that. I was wondering if you'd—"

Suddenly, her emotions roared to life. My words had obviously ignited something in her. "That's sure what it sounded like to me. Who do you think you are, coming on my property like this and accusing me—?"

"Ma'am, I'm not accusing you. I'm just trying to start a conversation. I was hoping you may have seen something." That sounded reasonable, didn't it? It was too bad this woman was far from reasonable at this moment in time.

Her gaze turned even frostier. "You say they're missing?"

I nodded, hoping something would be revealed in this conversation and it wouldn't be a total waste of our efforts. Our time was running out quickly. "That's correct."

"Good. I didn't take them, but I applaud whoever did it." She crossed her arms defiantly.

"Why would you applaud them?" I asked, perplexed and maybe even flabbergasted.

"They're nothing but a nuisance."

"The reindeer? How do they even affect you?"

"The reindeer themselves, not so much. But all of the hubbub next door is nothing but a headache. Do you know that during Christmas, it can take my family two hours to get to our driveway? Cars are lined up for miles down that road. We can't cut through in the opposite lane because it's a two-lane road with steep drop offs. It would be a death wish, so we have no choice but to either stay inside on those days, or wait in line to get to our home. One year we even ran out of gas while backed up in that traffic. You can imagine what fun that was."

"I can see where that would be frustrating," Chad said, pulling his lips into a tight line.

"More than frustrating. It makes me miserable at Christmas. Life is complicated enough without adding that headache."

"Hey, it's the candy hooker lady and her bearded friend," a small voice said. "Did you come to get my message for Santa?"

My eyes widened as the little boy we'd met on the sidewalk yesterday appeared in the doorway. His eyes looked as innocent as ever, making it hard to be mad at him and his quirky little remarks.

The woman—his mother, I assumed—didn't acknowledge his comment. "Charlie, please let me talk. Run along and play."

As soon as Charlie sauntered off, Mrs. Nimble stared at us, daring us to challenge her anymore.

"So, you're saying you didn't take the reindeer?" I repeated, never one to back down from confrontation.

"What would we do with a flock of reindeer?" she asked.

A herd, I silently corrected. *A herd*.

"Besides, we don't have a trailer to take them anywhere," the woman continued. "It would be much easier to pull down the Davis' lights, cut electricity to their place, or give Santa food poisoning. Stealing reindeer would be way too complicated."

She had a point.

But that still didn't give me any answers.

She leaned closer and lowered her voice. "One more thing. I don't even like Christmas!" Venom dripped from her voice.

"How can you not like Christmas?" I asked, my voice raspy with surprise. I wasn't sure where my question had come from. Maybe I truly had been infected with Christmas spirit.

"Because Santa can't help me. Jesus can't either. The whole notion of Christmas only gives my boy false hope. No hope is better than false hope."

My heart panged with sadness. "I'm . . . I'm sorry."

I didn't know what else to say. I didn't know the woman well enough to offer a hug or even advice.

I'd only recently started going to church, so I didn't even have any spiritual insight.

"Thank you for your time," Chad said, his hand on my elbow as he pulled me away.

Just as he led me down the porch, Charlie yelled from the window, "Bring some more candy . . . candy—hookers!—with you next time you come. And let me know if you decide to talk to Santa . . . or Jesus!"

***

"That poor boy," I murmured as I climbed into Chad's Vanagon. "His mom doesn't like Christmas. I wonder what's going on."

"Maybe they don't feel like they have any reason to celebrate."

I nodded as a weight pressed on my heart. "Maybe. I just hate to hear that they have no hope. I don't know what their circumstances are, but that just sounds incredibly sad."

I'd come a long way since I started writing a book called *Stupid People*. Maybe my compassion for animals was finally spilling over into empathy for people as well. Or maybe it was my pregnancy. My marriage? The fact that I'd started going to church? I couldn't be sure.

"We still have a few days here. Maybe we can think of a way to spread Christmas cheer before we leave," Chad said.

"Yeah, maybe." I let out a long sigh. "So, where does this leave us?"

Chad shrugged. "I'm not sure. No one knows anything about what happened to the reindeer or has seen anything. Which is strange. "

"That means either people aren't telling the truth or something very strange occurred. I just can't imagine what."

We sat there in silence for a minute.

"I think I know what happened!" Chad said, smacking his hand on the steering wheel.

My heart rate quickened. "Really? What?"

He stared at me, dead serious. "I think Santa magically transported the reindeer to the North Pole. I bet Rudolph wasn't feeling well, and he needed some back-ups."

I set my jaw and looked away.

"Just joking. JK!" He lilted his voice, purposefully sounding like a teenage girl. His grin slipped but a goofy expression remained. "LOL?"

"You're such a dork sometimes." I couldn't resist a chuckle.

"Yet you love me anyway."

"Okay, in all seriousness, the Christmas

celebration starts tonight, and Christmas is only three days away. I know this light show means a lot to your family, and they're counting on us to help them out."

"I thought you didn't even approve of people using animals for entertainment purposes, among other things." He stared at me, his eyes narrowed with curiosity.

"I don't. But I sense that your family sees them as more than animals. They seem to think of these reindeer as family. Plus, I fear these poor creatures are suffering a far worse fate than being introduced to the community in an annual holiday tradition."

"I love your passion, Sierra. I really do. And thank you for giving my family the benefit of the doubt. I appreciate it." He planted a kiss on my lips.

"Funny how life has changed since last year at this time, isn't it?" I said. "Who would have ever thought we'd be married today with a baby on the way? Certainly not me, but I'm glad we're here."

He nodded. "Me too. Now, I guess we should get back to finding those reindeer."

CHAPTER 8

Back at the house, I felt I was at an impasse. If Sam Bills, the animal rights activist, didn't take the reindeer, and the crazy neighbors who resented the whole Christmas "spectacle" didn't do it, then I had no idea who might. Sheriff Orlando didn't like the Davises, but that didn't give him enough motivation to break the law he'd pledged to uphold by stealing animals.

I needed to rethink my strategy.

Chad and I grabbed some sandwiches and chips to refuel before we continued with our investigation. Well, Chad had sandwiches and chips. I had hummus with carrots and celery. Everyone else was outside putting last minute touches on the display.

"Chad, could you call Vernon and confirm that Sam Bills was at the hardware store yesterday, trying to fix his washing machine like he said?" I asked, sticking a carrot in my mouth.

"I'm on it." He picked up his cell phone and

79

swallowed quickly before someone answered. A few minutes later, Chad hung up. "Vernon checked with all of his employees. No one saw Sam Bills at the hardware store. Apparently, they think Sam is hysterical because he gets wound up so easily. They purposely say things to get a rise out of him."

It definitely sounded like everyone there would remember if Sam came in.

That meant the man didn't have an alibi.

"He seems crazy enough that he might just plan a hijinks like this," Chad said. "One other thing Vernon said that I thought was interesting. Apparently, Sam Bills and Sheriff Orlando are cousins."

"Really?" Did that have anything to do with this? I wasn't sure, but I stored that information away as we finished lunch.

I was getting desperate, which meant I needed to hold on to every remote possibility.

***

Chad got roped into helping string up some more lights after lunch. While he did that, I walked over to the gate leading into the reindeer pen to check those tire tracks one more time. I squatted down to get a better look at them.

Had someone waited for the family to leave, backed up a trailer, and hauled away all of the animals? That took quite a bit of guts. It was a big risk, especially in the middle of the day.

Which made it even stranger that no one had seen anything.

"You know anything about tire tracks?" Paula asked, appearing behind me with a steaming mug of coffee in her hands. "That would be a handy talent to have right about now."

I stood and tightened the scarf around my neck. It certainly was chilly out here. It felt like . . . well, it felt like Christmas.

"I wish I did. These tracks are pretty deep. Maybe that means it was a heavy truck? It would have to be heavy to leave any marks with the ground so hard like it is," I mused aloud. "The trailer rules out the Nimbles."

"What do you mean?" She tilted her head.

I shrugged. "If the family doesn't have a trailer, they couldn't have left these tracks, and therefore, they couldn't have stolen the reindeer."

"But the Nimbles *do* have a trailer," Paula said.

"Come again?" I couldn't have heard her correctly. I shook my head, just to make sure nothing was clogging up my ears and causing me to not understand.

She nodded. "They sell Christmas trees in town. How else would they get the trees down to Main Street?"

Outrage rushed through me. Mrs. Nimble had lied to me? And I'd fallen for it?

Despicable.

"They own that Christmas tree lot? But they hate Christmas." My words sounded weak, even to my own ears.

"That's what they say. They're just kind of grumpy. It's a shame, really," Paula continued with a shake of her head. "That little Charlie is the cutest little guy. He climbs over to that ridge over there and just watches everything. I make sure he has some extra time with Santa when he sneaks over for the light show, too."

"Charlie seems like quite the character. But what's the family's problem?"

"I don't know. They don't want anything to do with us. It's been that way since they moved here a few years ago." She shrugged. "You can't make everyone happy, can you?"

"No, you certainly can't."

"It's a real shame. In this world today, people need something to look forward to. You know why we don't charge for the light show?"

"I have no idea."

She leaned against the fence post, her eyes serious. Unfortunately, since she wore reindeer antlers, her voice and her look were at odds. "When we started doing this fifteen years ago, the local factory had just closed. People didn't have any money. They didn't have any hope. We wanted to do something to cheer them up."

"O Come All Ye Faithful" began playing through the overhead speakers as we chatted.

"Tell me more."

"Paul and I didn't start with a lot. We'd just bought this property. It wasn't much at the time. There was just a little shack and a whole lot of possibilities. As we grew our home, we added to the show each year. At first, all of this was just for us. Then friends came over and told us how much they enjoyed it. We decided to open our property to the public. We couldn't believe the response. It's grown into what it is today."

"That sounds wonderful." I pressed my lips together as determination solidified itself in my gut. "I haven't given up on finding them, Aunt Paula. Is there anyone else you can think of who might want to get rid of them?"

She tapped her finger against her lips in thought. "You know, just last night I had another idea. I almost hated to say it because I don't want to accuse anyone. But the man who used to own the reindeer—the man who abandoned them—is back in town. His name is Henry Jones."

"Tell me more."

"I guess he's always thought the reindeer were rightfully his. I heard rumor he found another job and bought some more land not too long ago."

My pulse spiked. We had another lead. "I'll grab Chad and we can check it out."

"Those reindeer are out there somewhere, Sierra. I hope a lead turns up sometime."

"Me too," I told her grimly. "Me too."

***

An hour later, Chad and I pulled up to Henry Jones' house. He lived on a piece of secluded property in the mountains. His place wasn't big, but it was a well maintained, two-story brick house.

Chad and I knocked on the door, but no one answered. It wasn't really surprising considering that most people were working and others were traveling out of town for the holidays.

"There goes that lead, huh?" Chad muttered as we stepped off the porch. "I hate to say it, but I don't think we're going to find those reindeer before the show opens tonight."

I raised my chin, too stubborn to give up yet. "Want to take a walk back there?" I nodded toward the back of his property.

"We'd be trespassing."

"No one's here. It shouldn't hurt just to take a peek back there. I just want to see what's beyond the barn."

He hesitated another moment before finally saying, "I suppose just a peek can't hurt anything."

We tromped across the grass toward a barn in the background. It wasn't so much the barn that fascinated me, as it was the fenced in area behind the structure. I knew it was a long shot, but that fence looked new. It could be a place where cattle or sheep were kept, I supposed. But what if he had other plans for that area?

I wanted to see for myself, so that when we left his property I'd have no doubt in my mind.

By the time we reached the barn, I was out of breath.

"Maybe you should take it easy," Chad said, his hand on my back. "Maybe you're pushing this too hard. I should have insisted you stay at the house and rest. This is too much for you."

I brushed him off. "Don't be silly. This isn't too much. I'm just not used to the altitude or the hills."

"Are you sure you're okay? I don't want to do anything to put you or the baby in danger. If anything happened to either of you, I'd never forgive myself. I'd never *deserve* to forgive myself."

I laid my hand on his chest. "Chad, you're overreacting. I'm fine. This simply proves that I need to get more exercise." It was one of the hazards of working a desk job. I was an administrator now, which meant more paperwork and less time on my feet.

I sucked in a breath and straightened, knowing that if I didn't do something soon to show that I was okay, Chad would haul me back to his aunt and uncle's place, and I'd be on bed rest for the rest of my stay. I couldn't let that happen.

Suddenly, something moved from behind the barn.

It was a . . . reindeer?

CHAPTER 9

"Arrest them! They're on my property!" Henry Jones accused, pointing his finger at Chad and I.

"What did you do with the other ten reindeer?" I asked, craning my neck to see if there were any more reindeer hidden somewhere.

Sheriff Orlando refereed the two of us, putting his hands out like we might get into a fistfight. Chad and I had called the sheriff to come as soon as we'd spotted the two reindeer. Unfortunately, Sheriff Orlando and Henry Jones had pulled up at the same time, which had led to this confrontation.

"What other ten reindeer? I only have two." Henry Jones glowered at me.

He was probably in his fifties with pointy features and a ruddy complexion. He was none too happy to come home and find us here.

"You stole these from the Davises!" I snapped back.

"That's ridiculous. Why would I do something like that?"

I turned to the sheriff. "He would do it because the reindeer at the Davis' property used to be his. He abandoned the animals, the Davises rescued them, and now he's bitter."

"I applaud them for taking care of my reindeer!" Henry insisted.

"See!" I started, before my thoughts ground to a halt. "Wait. What?"

"I said, I applaud them. It broke my heart to leave those reindeer behind, but I had no other choice. It was either feed my children or feed my reindeer."

"You could have done something with them. Taken them somewhere safe. Left them in someone else's care."

"I tried! No one wants reindeer. I didn't know what to do with them. I figured maybe they could survive out here on their own. I know it sounds cruel, but when you're desperate you make yourself believe whatever you need to believe to cope."

"So, whose reindeer are these?" I pointed to the field.

"These are my reindeer. I just got them last week. Now that I'm back on my feet again, I wanted to start over."

"What do you do with these reindeer, Henry?"

Sheriff Orlando asked.

"I enjoy them. I watch them graze. I hope to take them to local schools and help educate children about them. But that's it."

"Can I see your paperwork confirming the sales of these animals, sir?" Orlando asked. "That could clear all of this up easily."

"Of course. I'll go get that right now." The man scowled at me one last time before stomping into his house. We all waited there silently for him to return. What was there to say? If I was wrong—and it was looking that way—then I'd flubbed up royally. But could anyone blame me? On the outside, who would have thought that two families in town might have reindeer? The thought was ridiculous.

Of course, the fact was that truth was often stranger than fiction.

Henry stomped back outside with something in his hands. I wanted to see those papers, but I let Sheriff Orlando do his job.

He took his precious time scanning the documents. Finally, he nodded, handed the papers to Henry, and then stepped back. "This is all legit," he said. "I'm sorry, sir, for the misunderstanding. Would you like to press charges for trespassing?"

Henry glared at me, and I held my breath. He

very well could do that, and I wouldn't blame him. But I really didn't want to go through the hassle of being arrested for something this silly.

"No, I'll let it drop this time," he finally said. "But only because I'm feeling the holiday spirit. No other reason."

Relief washed through me. Thank goodness.

"But don't ever show up here again," he warned. "If you do, I may not be as nice next time. I'll go the naughty route."

"We'll be going now." Chad led me away before I could get into any more trouble. We were halfway to our van when a voice called out to us.

"I need a word with you two." Sheriff Orlando briskly walked toward us. His cheeks were rosy and full, but his gaze appeared full of suspicion.

"I heard you two have been asking a lot of questions around town," he started.

"Someone has to," I retorted.

Chad nudged me gently, a silent reminder to watch my tongue lest we end up in jail.

"I'll have you know that my men and I have been asking our own questions about those reindeer. We're taking this very seriously."

"I guess you haven't had any more luck than we have," I said, trying to keep my voice easy. It was so hard, though!

"No one knows anything." He paused for a minute, his jaw twitching. "Will the light show still go on?"

"You better believe it!" I burst. Chad nudged me again, and I tried to simmer.

"This light show is important," Chad said. "Of course we'd love to have the reindeer there, but the show will still take place whether we do or not. It's important for the morale of the community."

He nodded slowly, almost defiantly. "Is that right?"

Just then, something caught my eye. I crept closer to the sheriff, my eyes focused on his shirt. "What's that?"

He took a step back, his hardened expression softening with surprise. "Excuse me?"

Without thinking, I picked a hair off his sleeve and held it to the light. "Is this a . . . reindeer hair?"

The sheriff opened his mouth and then shut it again. Finally, he said, "That's ridiculous."

I examined the hair again. "No, reindeer have hollow hair follicles that keep them insulated in cold weather. Some people even believe that reindeer hair is magical. Without tests, I can't say anything for certain, but I'm willing to bet my Christmas wishes that this is reindeer hair. And I know for a fact that you didn't actually get near Mr. Jones' animals back there."

"What are you implying, young lady?"

"I'm implying that you have a major grudge against the Davis family. Maybe you even got your cousin Sam Bills involved, and you two took those reindeer yourself in order to devastate the Davises."

"That's an awfully big accusation. Are you sure you want to go there?" His jaw twitched.

Chad grabbed my arm as if he feared I might sock the sheriff. I wouldn't go that far. The sheriff wasn't worth it.

I narrowed my eyes. "What did you do with those animals, Sheriff?"

He practically had steam coming from his nostrils as he stared down at me. "I'm a sworn officer of the law. I didn't do anything with those animals."

"Then explain this!" I raised the hair as if it were a sword. A miniature sword made for fairies to fight with.

"I can't," he said. "But I'd suggest you back off before you get yourself in trouble."

I shook my head. "I'm not dropping this. If you think I'm that weak spirited, then you're about to be in for a rude awakening."

With that, I climbed into the Vanagon and slammed the door.

The sheriff had something to do with those reindeer disappearing. I just had to figure out what.

CHAPTER 10

When we got back to Paul and Paula's, I was fuming inside. How would I ever prove that the sheriff and Sam Bills were behind this? Sam had a trailer and no alibi, so he had the means and the opportunity. The sheriff had motive: he wanted to ruin the Davises. Without finding the reindeer, however, I had no proof.

I needed to find out where the sheriff lived and see if he had enough property to keep the reindeer there.

I found Paula outside where she was handing out cookies to her volunteers.

"Do you know where the sheriff lives?" I asked.

She stopped cookie delivery, her eyes widening. "He lives in town. Why?"

"Does he have a lot of property?"

"Maybe a half acre at the most. Why?"

"I think he may be behind your reindeer disappearing," I blurted.

"What? Orlando?" She gasped, her hand going

over her heart. "No. He wouldn't take things that far."

"He had reindeer hair on him, and he obviously dislikes the family," Chad added.

"But, maybe there's another explanation."

I shrugged. "Maybe. But you're sure he couldn't keep the reindeer at his house?"

She nodded. "I'm positive. There's just not enough property."

I sighed and leaned back, wondering where to go next.

"Sierra, if we don't find the reindeer before tonight, I understand. You've given this your best." Paula frowned and handed me a cookie. "Cookies always make me feel better."

"Thank you." I stared down at the reindeer sugar cookie and my stomach grumbled. I ignored it. "I don't want to give up. I want to find those reindeer, now more than ever."

"I know, dear. I know." She patted my arm. "I've got to go finish stringing up a few more lights. Chad, can you help?"

Chad glanced at me one more time. "Of course. Are you going to be okay, Sierra?"

I nodded. "Yeah, I'll be fine. I'm just going to go walk to the reindeer pen again."

I needed some time alone to think.

"Oh yes, take it easy, darling," Paula said. "You don't want to push yourself too hard."

I trudged back toward the stables, trying to sort out my thoughts. What was I missing? Was there some angle I hadn't considered? A suspect I hadn't pondered?

It had to be the sheriff. He was the only one who made sense. Besides, he acted like he was hiding something. But where would Sheriff Orlando have taken the reindeer? And why would he risk his career for this?

As I paused by the fence, I saw Uncle Paul walking my way. His shoulders looked tight, and even from where I stood, I could see the deep lines around his mouth and forehead. I wondered if he'd gotten bad news about the reindeer. I hoped not.

"Hi, Uncle Paul."

He stopped beside me. "Sierra. I was hoping to find you out here."

"Is everything okay?"

He rubbed his beard a moment and sucked in a deep breath. "I just got back in from town. I ran into Sheriff Orlando."

I crossed my arms and scowled, remembering my earlier conversation with the man. The sheriff must have shared that I'd been trespassing. There was nothing like having a blabbermouth for sheriff.

"I guess he told you?"

Paul's frown deepened. "Yes, he did."

"That man has a lot of nerve. I just don't trust him."

"He told me that you're an animal rights activist."

My thoughts crashed, nearly shutting me down for a moment. "Did he?"

"I have a question for you, Sierra."

"Sure. Anything." Anxiety grew in my stomach. Something didn't feel right, but I was trying not to read too much into things.

"You got to our house early, right? While the rest of us had gone into town?"

I nodded. "That's correct."

He shifted, looking like a weight pressed on his shoulders. "I don't want to start any trouble in the family. But Sierra, I have to ask this. Did you have anything to do with the reindeer disappearing?"

CHAPTER 11

All the blood drained from my face. "No, I didn't have anything to do with this. I promise. I would never do that to your family."

I wanted to explain how I'd bent over backward in order not to offend anyone. I'd even eaten broth made from the meat of animals! I'd tried to rescue animals only so they could be put back into captivity. Didn't he see the sacrifice that required from me?

"I don't want to think the worst in anyone," Uncle Paul continued. "I really don't. But I know about Paws and Furballs and all of their past campaigns."

"This isn't one of my campaigns, though. You're family." Panic started to rise in me.

"I found this in your vest pocket." He held up the bell I'd found downtown. "I wasn't going through your things, but I went to hang it up after it fell off the hook by the front door. The bell fell out when I did."

"I can explain that. I found it on the ground when I was walking around. I thought it was litter so I picked it up."

"It belongs to my reindeer. They all wore bells."

"I had no idea. I promise you. I just found it. You've got to believe me."

He frowned. "I want to. I really do. It's just that nasty email you sent us. It makes me see a different side of your personality, makes me think you're hiding something."

"Nasty email? I've never sent you any nasty emails." What in the world was he talking about?

"Well, your company has. They've sent emails about the reindeer to Paula and I, and I just received one today about my company, as a matter of fact. Imagine my surprise when your name was on it."

"Your company?"

"Good Day Fishing Hooks."

I gawked, feeling like I'd been punched in the gut. "You own Good Day Fishing Hooks?"

"I thought you knew?"

I shook my head. "I had no idea. And Paws and Furballs didn't send you any letters. A man named Sam Bills sent them. He's one of our supporters and he used our name in the letter, but we did not endorse it."

His tepid gaze met mine. "I suppose you have an excuse about the email I got a few minutes ago also?"

"My assistant must have drafted it, but she wasn't supposed to send anything. You've got to believe me! I had no idea that was even your company."

Paul looked at me, hurt and accusation evident in his usually jolly eyes. "I just hope for Chad's sake that you didn't have anything to do with this. It would break his heart."

As he walked away, I sagged against the fence, unable to ignore the implications of what had just happened. How could they think I'd be behind this? Then I remembered my past escapades. I supposed if this wasn't Chad's family then there might have been a slight possibility I would do something like this. I had done some crazy things before, even freeing crabs at an oceanfront restaurant once.

Only adding to my dismal thoughts was the fact that the song on the overhead switched from "Joy to the World" to "You're a Mean One, Mr. Grinch." I felt like the Grinch at the moment.

I knew I had no choice but to leave here. It wasn't that I wanted to run away. But I wouldn't be welcome any longer.

Sadness pressed on my heart at the thought.

So much for my dreams of fitting in with the family.

How was I going to break this news to Chad? And why hadn't he told me about Good Day Fishing Hooks?

There was one thing I had to settle in my mind before I left. I pulled out my cell phone. I had to know if Cindy sent that email. Thankfully, she answered on the first ring.

"Cindy, please tell me you didn't send anything to Good Day Fishing Hooks?" I started, despair evident in my voice.

"Of course not. You told me not to without your approval."

"The owner said he received correspondence from us today."

"Oh, Sierra. I didn't send anything." Computer keys tapped in the background again. "See, there's the email right there in my draft fold—" She gasped. "Oh my goodness. It's not in my draft folder anymore. Somehow I accidentally sent it, Sierra. I'm so sorry. I have no idea how this happened."

"Cindy, I understand you're sorry, but this has caused an avalanche of other issues." I sighed and shook my head.

"I'm so sorry, Sierra. I really am. I'm

CHRISTY BARRITT

flabbergasted at this mistake!"

"Don't worry about it, Cindy." My voice sounded as dull as I felt. "I need to run. We'll talk about it later."

I shook my head, unable to believe my horrible luck. There was nothing I could do about it now, though.

I glanced in the distance at everyone as they laughed together and continued to string lights. My heart lurched and ached. I wished things had turned out differently.

I gave one last glance down at the tire tracks by the gate. I still didn't understand how someone had driven through town with those reindeer without anyone seeing anything.

What was I missing?

I froze.

What if that was because no one had driven through town? Or through the back roads even, for that matter?

What if someone had simply released them into the wild? I supposed that was a possibility, though part of me sensed that the animals would have returned. This property was their source of food, and they'd likely gravitate back toward the area for that reason alone, if nothing else.

I squatted down one more time. In between

the gravel, I spotted a speck of white. I carefully pulled it out.

Popcorn, I realized.

I glanced up at the mountain as it stretched upward into the sky. Staying low to the ground, I walked away from the gate.

Sure enough, a few more feet away, I found another piece. This one looked like it was caramel flavored.

The reindeer's favorite. That's what Aunt Paula had said.

As I reached the edge of the woods, I paused and squatted. There, underneath some underbrush, was yet another piece of popcorn.

Strange.

Why was there popcorn out here?

I gazed around. In the distance, I spotted more pieces. What was this? A spinoff of the candy trail that Hansel and Gretel had left?

I didn't know.

Despite that, I found myself following the line of popcorn. I had to see where it led.

CHAPTER 12

I paused to look back as I neared the crest of the mountain. I was farther away from the house than I'd expected to be. I didn't want to wander too far from the property. Honestly, part of me just wanted to get out of town. But first I had to see where this trail led.

Before I turned back around, I spotted Chad walking my way, waving me down.

I frowned as I waited for him. When he joined me, he frowned also, his husband radar obviously kicking in.

"What's going on?" he asked.

I cut right to the chase. "Why didn't you tell me that your uncle owned a company that manufactures fish hooks?"

His shoulders sagged. "I wanted to. I did. But I knew you'd both have bad impressions of each other. I wanted you to get to know each other first."

"And then form bad impressions?" I squawked.

He shook his head, rubbing his forehead with frustration. "No, that's not what I meant."

"Then what did you mean?"

He let out a long sigh. "I've really messed this up. I'm sorry, Sierra. I started to tell you about my uncle's company right before that deer appeared in the road."

"Uncle Paul thinks I might be behind the disappearance of the reindeer. I forgot how quickly word gets around in small towns. It's working against me that I arrived early while the rest of you were gone. I have no alibi, I have motive, and I suppose I could have had one of my employees pull up a trailer, which would give me the means as well. I look guiltier than any of the other suspects we've talked to."

He stepped back. "I should go talk to Uncle Paul. I'll tell him this is all my fault. If I'd just been upfront from the beginning—"

"No, don't. His assumptions are natural. I'm just disappointed because I wanted your family to like me." Tears stung my eyes at the thought. I wasn't normally a crier, but my hormones were all out of whack with this pregnancy. I could cry at commercials even, especially those sentimental ones the card companies put out. Even a coffee commercial had done me in last week.

"Of course they like you, Sierra."

"Let's be honest, Chad. I'm not the most likable person. I'm much better with animals than humans. My passion for what I do sometimes supersedes the rules of political correctness and social graces."

"You mean you're outspoken sometimes?"

I nodded. "Yes, that's what I mean."

"So, you're being yourself. You're being who you were created to be. Some people just can't accept people who aren't afraid to be real."

I wiped the tears from my eyes. "I feel like I ruined this trip. I know you were looking forward to introducing me to your family."

He pulled me into a hug and rubbed my back. "Of course you didn't ruin it. You've gone above and beyond. I'm the one who ruined things. I messed up royally this time." He leaned down until we were eye to eye. "Do you want to leave?"

Everything in me screamed, "Yes!" I did want to take off and get out of here. But I was stronger than that. "No, not until I follow this popcorn."

"What are you talking about?"

I explained to him what I was doing.

"So, you're following a trail of food?" he clarified. "You remember what happened when Hansel and Gretel did this? Their results were less than stellar."

"Look, I know it sounds strange, but it's true. It's what happened." I pointed to another piece. "That popcorn looks kind of fresh, don't you think? And why is there popcorn in the woods?"

Chad held my hand as we hiked through the mountains. It felt good to know he was by my side, even through all the misunderstandings and flub ups. He'd forgiven me for the whole incident at my family's house, so I knew I couldn't hold a grudge.

"The show starts in three hours."

"I know it will be great, Chad, despite everything that's happened."

But inside, I wasn't sure any of it would be great. I was feeling emotional and sensitive and not like myself. Part of it may have been the pregnancy, but the other part of it was probably some fears I'd had bottled deep inside of me. Fears of not being accepted by the people who mattered. Chad's family mattered.

We reached the top of the incline, and I continued to see a trail of popcorn. Interesting.

I wondered how many people knew those reindeer liked popcorn. Had someone tried to lure them away?

"Look, the trail leads all the way down there." Chad pointed to a clearing in the distance.

I squinted. "Is that . . . the Nimbles' property?"

"You know what? It very well could be. Let's go check it out."

CHAPTER 13

Going downhill was much easier than going uphill, except for my knees, which ached under the strain of walking down the steep grade. I held Chad's hand to keep my balance.

We reached the edge of the tree line, and the old dilapidated barn from the Nimbles' property appeared ahead.

Little Charlie played on the grass there . . . jingling a bell? A bell just like the one I'd found on the ground in downtown Oldsburgh, the one that had belonged to one of Paul and Paula's reindeer.

Before we could say anything, the boy spotted us. I braced myself for his greeting, knowing exactly what was coming. He surprised me with, "Hey, guys."

Hadn't Paula said that Charlie liked to climb up that ridge and watch the reindeer?

Everything was becoming all too clear in my mind.

"What's going on, Charlie?" Chad asked, his

hands going to his hips as he surveyed the area beyond Charlie.

Guilt seeped into the boy's eyes. "Nothing. Why?"

I squatted down so I could look him in the eye—and maybe seem less intimidating. "Charlie, did you leave that trail of caramel corn through the woods?"

I saw the truth in his eyes. Yes, he had left it. But, instead of owning up to it, he shook his head. "No. Why would you ask that?"

Chad leaned down closer. "Are you sure, Charlie?"

He nodded, his shoulders drooping. He glanced behind him at the barn, suddenly looking nervous. "Why would I do that?"

"Maybe to lure the reindeer away from their home?" I asked.

His chin trembled, and he dropped the bell. It hit the ground with a half-hearted jangle. "Please don't tell the police! I don't want to go to jail. I didn't mean anything bad."

"We're not sending you to jail, Charlie," I assured him. "Can you just tell us what's going on? We've been very worried."

A tear rolled down his cheek, but he quickly wiped it away and held his chin up. "I'm sorry. I just needed those reindeer."

"Why would you need the reindeer?" I asked, unable to imagine any reason for a child to *need* reindeer.

"Because my dad doesn't have a job. If he doesn't find one soon, we're going to be homeless," Charlie said. "He hurt himself while shoveling some snow, and he can't do construction any more. Mom always looks sad, and dad is always trying to find odd jobs, so I don't see him a lot."

"I'm so sorry to hear that, Charlie," I told him. And I was. But I'd address that in a minute. "But what does that have to do with the reindeer?"

"I've been begging Santa all year to give my dad a new job for Christmas. I thought Santa might need his reindeer early in order to go job-hunting for my dad. Santa wouldn't be able to go anywhere if the reindeer were being kept next door."

Chad and I exchanged a sad smile. How could anyone be upset after they heard that explanation? It was impossible.

"So you lured the reindeer out after you saw that everyone had left?" Chad clarified.

"I didn't mean any harm. I keep waiting for Santa to take them, but he hasn't yet." He looked up at the sky, as if he expected to see some elves and a man in a red suit suddenly appear.

"Where are the reindeer, Charlie?" I asked.

"They're in the barn. I've been feeding them every day and taking real good care of them."

"Have you been feeding them popcorn?" I asked.

He nodded. "But other things, too. Like hay. And I've given them water. I promise, I took really good care of them."

"Can we see them?" Chad asked.

Charlie nodded again. "Sure. Follow me."

We followed the boy into the barn. Sure enough, there were twelve reindeer there.

"Am I going to be in big trouble?" Charlie asked with a frown.

I squeezed his shoulder. "I think everyone will understand when we explain to them what happened."

"I'm going to call my uncle," Chad said, pacing away to a quiet corner.

Just then, the sheriff appeared in the doorway to the barn.

I moaned, realizing how this probably looked. I was here with the missing reindeer. The sheriff already disliked me. No one would think Charlie did this of his own freewill. I'd look just as guilty to the sheriff as I'd looked to Uncle Paul.

I didn't see accusation on his face, though. I saw . . . guilt?

"You knew the reindeer were here," I muttered.

"I was following up on a lead." He tugged at his shirt collar.

I shook my head. "No you weren't. You knew these reindeer were here. Just how long were you going to stay silent?"

He cringed again, his cheeks reddening. "You're accusing me of breaking the law?"

"Everyone in town knows you're still bitter because Paula chose Paul instead of you."

He stared at me a moment and then chuckled. "Is that what you think? I got over Paula a long time ago."

"Then why are you so bitter toward the family? What did they ever do to you?"

He stared off in the distance for a moment. "The Davises are like heroes in this town. He employs more than half of the county. He puts on this light show for free. He helps people in need. He can do no wrong!"

Pieces came together in my mind. "So, you found these reindeer when you came here to ask the Nimbles what they knew. They weren't home, you snooped and found them. But, instead of returning them, you waited until now. You wanted to be the hero for once."

The surprise on his face told me I was right. He sobered and nodded. "You have no evidence."

"How can you live with yourself? You're paid to uphold the law and this is what you do?"

His face cracked into a huge frown as he ran a hand over his brow. "You're right. I don't know what I was thinking. I was going to return the reindeer tonight. I really was."

"What about your cousin, Sam Bills?"

His frown deepened. "I may have encouraged him to lay like a dead fish in front of Paul Davis' factory. Again, I didn't mean any harm."

"You encouraged him to send those emails too, didn't you?" Everything was starting to make sense.

He wiped his brow again. "Guilty as charged. I just wanted to feel like the one who saved the day for once. I became obsessed with it."

"My reindeer!" a woman squealed behind us.

I turned and saw Paul and Paula running toward the animals. Once they reached the creatures, they inspected each of them, whispering sweet words in their ears and rubbing their heads.

"They're here?" Uncle Paul said. "But what about those tire prints?"

"Do you think maybe Willie left them when he dropped off that load of hay?" Aunt Paula asked.

"I suppose that's a possibility we should have considered earlier," Uncle Paul said. "All along someone walked the reindeer over the mountain and into this barn. Who would have thought? Sierra, I'm so sorry. Please forgive me."

"Forgive you for what?" Paula asked, looking clueless. Paul hadn't told her!

"It was a misunderstanding," I quickly said. "Nothing, really."

Paul pulled me into a hug. "Thank you so much. You just saved our Christmas." Then he whispered, "I'm sorry."

"No reason to be," I told him quietly.

He looked beyond me to Sheriff Orlando and stiffened. "Sheriff."

Orlando nodded back, looking equally as uncomfortable. "Paul."

"What? How . . .?" Paula started. "Why exactly are my reindeer here?"

I frowned and glanced over at little Charlie. "I guess his dad has been without a job. Charlie was hoping these reindeer would help Santa find some employment for his dad."

Paula gasped. "I had no idea!"

I nodded grimly. "It's heartbreaking, isn't it? I

guess selling Christmas trees helps to put some food on the table, but they can't pay their mortgage."

She grew silent for a moment. "I may just be able to help them. I'll need to talk to a few people first, though. Communities are supposed to look out for each other. We can't let this happen."

The sheriff nodded beside us. "I agree. We should help. I'll do whatever I can."

Paula nodded resolutely. "I promise that Charlie will have a good Christmas, if it's the last thing I do. But the show starts in an hour. In order to put my plan into action, I've got to get back there and make sure everything is ready. We have our reindeer, so we just need someone to play Santa."

"What happened to Santa?" Chad asked.

"He has a stomach bug," Paul said.

"I can fill in," Orlando said.

Everyone stopped and stared at him.

"You mean it?" Paula asked, stepping closer. "You'd do that?"

He nodded. "Of course I would. It's the least the sheriff could do to give back to his community."

"We'd love to have you help out, Orlando," Paula said. "Thank you. You're a real lifesaver."

He tipped his hat toward her. "No problem."

Finally, maybe he would get his chance to be the hero. I kept my mouth shut, deciding not to tell anyone that the sheriff had been aware of where the reindeer were. Call it Christmas cheer. Call it grace or compassion. But I had a feeling that everything would work out just the way it was supposed to.

CHAPTER 14

That evening, I donned my Mary costume. As I adjusted my headpiece in the mirror, I smiled at my reflection. I was actually looking forward to this.

The reindeer had been returned, Charlie had apologized, and everything was on track to make this a night of spectacular Christmas fun. I'd even had time to send Cindy an email, encouraging her not to worry about her mistake and asking her to send a "cease and desist" letter to Sam Bills, warning him not to use the Paws and Furballs name anymore or we would pursue legal action.

Just then, someone knocked on the door. I turned and saw Paula peeking in. "Can we talk?"

I sucked in a deep breath. "Sure."

She walked into my room and sat on the edge of the bed. "I just wanted to say thank you again. You may have single handedly just saved Christmas for this town."

"Now you're exaggerating, but you're welcome." My grin disappeared. "What about

Charlie? What's going to happen to him?"

"We won't press charges, of course. In fact, Paul just headed to the Christmas tree stand downtown to talk to Mr. Nimble. I wish we'd known about their struggles, but the family always kept to themselves."

"It sounds like things have been rough for the family."

"Paul is willing to offer Mr. Nimble a position with Good Day Fishing Hooks," Paula said. "We're also going to give all the money raised from the pie sales to the Nimbles. They'll have a good Christmas after all—at least we hope so."

"That's wonderful, Paula. Truly."

She pulled me into a hug of polar bear proportions. "We need to get outside and get in place. Are you ready for this?"

"I'm more than ready. I'm excited."

I stepped out into a wonderland. The lights on the front of the house flashed, blinked, and changed colors to the tune of "Up on the Housetop." Cars were already lined up down the road, and volunteers were rushing around to get everything in place. Even better—a sprinkling of snow had begun to fall from the sky, making everything look like a giant snowglobe.

I met Chad at the manger and picked up the

baby doll that lay there. Something clutched my heart as I hugged the doll to my chest. Maybe it was longing for my own child? Excitement for the future? The promise of new beginnings and the chance to have the family I'd never had growing up?

"Everything okay?" Chad asked.

I nodded, tracing the baby's cheek. "Yeah, everything's great."

As I stood there, adjusting my headpiece once more, I heard a commotion in the backyard. I looked over and saw Mrs. Nimble rush toward Paula, throwing her arms around her. "Thank you so much!"

My heart warmed. In fact, it may have even grown. Similar to the Grinch's when the whole town started to sing "Welcome Christmas."

I squeezed the baby closer to my chest, feeling like I was at some kind of dress rehearsal for being a mom. Not just at this very moment, but all weekend as I'd learned to navigate family relations and children and hormones.

"You're going to be a great mom, you know," Chad said.

My smile faltered. "I'm not sure about that. Facing a Fortune 500 company about the mistreatment of animals seems a lot less scary than being a mom."

"You're going to be great. Someone who cares that much about animals? I have no doubt that you're going to care even more about a baby."

Tears glistened in my eyes. "You mean it?"

He nodded. "Yeah, I really do."

I gave him a quick kiss. "Thanks, Chad."

I looked around at the nativity, especially as the Wise Men and Shepherds began walking toward us. Something about the scene was beautiful, so much more eloquent than Santa and his reindeer could ever be.

"What are you thinking?" Chad asked.

"This nativity . . . it feels hopeful somehow. I don't know—maybe because hope began with a baby?"

"Hope is something everyone needs, isn't it? You're right. It all began with a baby who offers way more hope than Santa ever could."

Just then, Charlie came running over dressed in a tunic and head covering. "Hey, guys! Guess what? I get to be a shepherd." He held out his shepherd's staff. "Check out this hooker!"

Chad and I shared a laugh.

Chad planted a kiss on my lips. "Merry Christmas, Sierra."

My heart felt warm and full. "A merry

Christmas it is."

###

Check out Sierra's next adventure in: Rattled!

Keep reading for a preview.

Rattled

CHAPTER 1

"So, what exactly is the problem?" I pushed my glasses up higher on my nose and gently bounced my three-month-old son on my shoulder as my intern, Mandee Melkins, paused outside a tattered apartment door.

The college-aged girl pressed her thin lips together in apprehension as she fiddled with the key in the lock. Since I'd known Mandee, she'd always acted nervous and often too eager to please. She'd just started working with me a month ago at Animal Protective Services, formerly called Paws and Fur Balls, an animal rights nonprofit, and was already driving me crazy.

Mandee's request for me to meet her here today had almost pushed me over the edge. She had a tendency to be high maintenance, asking for way too much clarification on every assignment I'd given her. She often lingered, waiting for my approval—and praise—on everything she did. She worked late just so she could talk to me, which, unfortunately, was the last thing I wanted.

I'd left the office to meet Mandee after she called me in a panic about thirty minutes ago. She wouldn't tell me what was going on, only that she desperately needed my help and it couldn't wait and no one else would do.

So here I was. With my baby. With piles of paperwork waiting for me back at the office. At a strange apartment building probably ten minutes away from my own apartment in Norfolk, Virginia.

"Thanks for coming, Sierra. I can't describe my dilemma, exactly. It's better if you see for yourself." Mandee finally managed to unlock the door before shoving it open with a dramatic push. "To start with, I guess I should tell you that this isn't my place. I've been watching my friend Patrick's apartment while he's out of town."

I stepped inside behind her, wishing we could speed all of this up. Times like this—my impatient times—made me question how good a mother I was going to be. Weren't mothers supposed to be exceedingly patient and nurturing? I wasn't sure I'd earned those titles yet, and that scared me as I thought about the future. I only wanted the best for Reef.

CHRISTY BARRITT

The inside of Patrick's apartment smelled like animals and dirty socks and microwaved meals. And Patrick was obviously a slob because trash littered every available surface and made me not want to touch anything. Mandee was a better person than me for agreeing to stay here.

The only things about the apartment that had any appeal were the huge framed photos on the walls. A close-up of a lizard's eye, mysterious and haunting. A snake's upraised head as he stared at something unknown in the distance. A frog with his tongue extended toward a fly on the rock in front of him.

"Patrick loves snakes," Mandee continued. "All reptiles and amphibians, for that matter. He thinks they're super-duper adorable." As if to confirm it, she leaned toward an aquarium in the living room, where some aquatic frogs swam, and made a baby face at them. "Because you all are."

I wanted to roll my eyes.

I'd hired Mandee after reading her uber-impressive résumé. At age fourteen, she'd not only started a citywide campaign in her hometown of Annapolis, Maryland, where she'd raised $10,000 for a local animal shelter, but she'd also collected a whole truckload of dog food, bowls, beds, and more.

She continued with her campaign until she graduated from high school, and now she was studying business with the hopes of becoming a full-time fundraiser for animal-worthy causes. The achievement was definitely something to take note of. In my postpartum rush, I'd hired her on her résumé alone.

Then I'd met her in person on her first day on the job. She looked more like a little girl than a junior in college. More often than not, she donned leggings, colorful Keds, and oversized T-shirts, usually in varying shades of pink or purple. Sometimes she wore her brown hair in braids with clips on the ends.

She had the personality to match her appearance. Despite my initial misgivings, I decided to stand by my hasty hiring decision. Someone who'd done so many good things couldn't be all that bad, right?

"So who is this Patrick guy, exactly? A friend? Family member?" I asked, still bouncing Reef on my shoulder.

"Just a friend. We were in crew together last spring, and we bonded over our love for animals."

"I understand." I'd bonded with many people over that common trait.

"Anyway, he's down in Costa Rica because he won a trip after entering a contest on the back of a cereal box or something. He's down in the rain forest, where there's no cell service. Can you imagine not having cell service—"

"Mandee," I interrupted. "Forget about the oyster and get to the pearl."

I hadn't used that expression in years. My dad used to say it all the time, and it drove me crazy.

Whatever the method or word choice, I had to get Mandee focused again. I wasn't sure how long Reef would stay quiet and happy, but I knew I was on borrowed time. At any moment now, he could start howling, wanting either food or sleep or having gas.

Little three-month-old boys weren't much different than their grown counterparts.

"Oh, right. This way." She led me down a short hallway and came to a stop in front of a room.

She seemed to hesitate a moment before pushing the door open. When she did, I spotted a dark room filled with various terrariums. There were probably ten of them on different tables and stands along the edges of the space. The one directly beside me had a gecko inside.

I sucked in a quick breath when I saw what was inside the rest of them.

Snakes. There were snakes in these glass enclosures. All kinds of snakes, at that. I recognized a few of them but wished I didn't.

I might fight for the rights of animals across the country—the world, for that matter—but snakes still gave me the creeps.

"This happened," Mandee said.

I glanced at the tank she pointed to. It was huge—and I do mean huge. If I had to guess, it held at least sixty gallons. "That's quite a terrarium."

"It's actually a vivarium."

I scowled and pulled Reef closer to me, choosing to let her correction slide. Respect for authority from my employees was important, but my time was more valuable than a reprimand right now. I didn't want to think about what had lived in that space. I might have a degree from Yale, but sometimes emotions still trumped education.

"What happened, Mandee?"

"A thirteen-foot lavender albino ball python was in there."

"What do you mean, it *was* in there?" A shiver rushed through me, and I held Reef closer.

Mandee frowned and shook her head, still staring at the empty tank. "Chalice was snug as a bug in her little glass house last night. I fed her, just like Patrick told me. Then I closed the door and assumed everything was as I left it. I didn't bother to check on the snakes again until after I got back from my last class. When I came in here, her enclosure was empty."

I glanced behind me this time, my thoughts filled with visions of an ugly snake eating my baby. I believed in animals being treated well . . . but I wasn't sure how I'd react if any animal ever put my baby in danger. I think I'd go all Mama Bear on the creature, and my career with APS would thus be over. Yet, it would be worth it if it meant protecting my son.

I had to stay focused here. I was the director of a national nonprofit. Respected in the field. I'd written papers and articles that had been published internationally.

This was no time to look weak or wishy-washy.

"Did you latch the lid?" I peered closer at the little hooks there.

Mandee squirmed. "They're broken. I didn't think it would be a big deal. I mean, if she got out, she'd stay in this room, right? Besides, Patrick must not have thought it was a very big deal because he didn't say anything."

Irritation rose in me, but when Reef cooed on my shoulder, the emotion dissipated. I kissed his head, mentally kicking myself for not leaving him at home. But Chad—my husband and Reef's dad—had a big construction job out in West Virginia that he was getting ready for today, and he couldn't have easily watched Reef either. I just wasn't ready to find a permanent sitter for my baby. He belonged with me. It was the way nature had intended, and no one was going to change my mind about that.

"Did you look everywhere for her?" I finally asked.

She nodded. "I looked all around the apartment. Kitchen cabinets. Under the couch. Even in my bed. She's nowhere. But it's strange because snakes like that can't just disappear. I mean, she has to be somewhere . . . unless a snake rapture happened."

I tried not to sigh. But Mandee drove me absolutely crazy with her cutesy sayings and her hunger to impress. I wanted to help her, but I was so tired, and I felt like everyone needed me. I was being pulled in too many different directions, and every route seemed important.

"You're sure she's not in the apartment?"

Mandee shrugged like she didn't have a

care in the world. "It's kind of hard to hide a snake like that."

"That's true," I conceded. "But she didn't just disappear. You're right about that. You didn't hear anything last night?"

She pushed her glasses up on her nose. I noticed that she'd gotten some plastic frames a couple of weeks ago that were almost like mine. It was probably a coincidence, but it was a little strange. The only real difference in our frames was that hers were pink.

What kind of respectable adult wore pink frames?

"No, not really," she said.

"What do you mean: not really?"

She shrugged, almost looking sheepish. "A local theater was doing an all-night marathon of *My Little Pony* cartoons. I only lasted until 3:30. I know it sounds weird. I wasn't sure if I should mention it."

I had so much I could say about that, but I kept it all to myself for the sake of remaining civil. "We've got a problem here, Mandee."

"That's why I called you." Mandee beamed. "You're the smartest person I know. If anyone can locate this snake, it's you."

Being up on a pedestal had both its perks

and its downfalls. This would be a downfall. Snake hunting wasn't at the top of my priority list.

I sighed and glanced around. "Was the window open?"

"Nope. Already checked. It was locked and secure. All the windows were."

"There are really so few options as to where she could have gone." I began pacing the room. Every time I passed one of the snakes, I shivered. Why anyone would want to keep one of these reptiles in their home was beyond me. They deserved to be in nature . . . far, far away from humans.

I paused by one of the terrariums. It rested on a stand against the wall, and a corn snake tried climbing up the glass inside. He wavered back and forth as if something invisible teased him.

Something on the floor behind the wooden base of the vivarium didn't look right.

"Look at this, Mandee." I pointed to the tight, narrow space between the stand and the wall.

She squeezed beside me and squatted for a better look.

"It's an AC vent." She said it dead serious, like I'd lost my mind.

I stopped myself before scowling at her.

"Exactly. But it's not on correctly."

She scooted the terrarium out of the way to get a better look. Sure enough, there was a six-inch gap where the wooden floor and the metal sides of the vent cover were supposed to meet.

"You don't think . . ." Mandee looked up at me, and her lips parted in horror.

"I think that's where the snake went," I told her bluntly.

"But that would mean . . ."

"That Chalice could be anywhere in this building." I cringed at the thought. A snake that large was nothing to be played with.

She fanned her face. "Oh, that's bad. That's really bad. I've got to find Chalice, Sierra!"

***

An hour later, Mandee and I had knocked on every door in the apartment complex. Five other residents checked their apartments and hadn't found anything unusual or frightening slithering through their space. I didn't think they realized just how large the snake was because everyone looked behind pillows and potted plants. I didn't bother to correct them; it was better if they didn't know what they were up against.

Only one person hadn't answered their door, and, unfortunately, it was located on the first floor right below Patrick's apartment. Sensibly speaking, this apartment was the most likely place for the snake to go while slithering through the ductwork.

"They could be at work," I said as we stood outside the door.

Mandee shrugged. "Could be."

"You know anything about whoever lives here?" Reef had fallen asleep, and right now he nestled against my chest, looking absolutely adorable. I could stare at him all day.

If only I didn't have to work or help find this snake.

Mandee shrugged again and frowned. "The guy's name is Tag. He's not very friendly. At least, that's been my impression when our paths have crossed. I really can't remember anything else about him."

"Look, like I said, he's probably at work. Why don't we walk outside and see if we can look into his apartment? If the snake's in there, maybe we'll see her. We can call the landlord and, with any luck, the snake will be gone before Tag gets home from work."

"I knew you'd know exactly what to do.

Thanks, Sierra!" She threw her arms around me and nearly woke up Reef.

Honestly, I wasn't much of a hugger. Even in the post-pregnancy hormonal craziness, I still wasn't a hugger. But I knew the sentiment behind Mandee's action was respectable. And Reef didn't wake up, so it was all good.

We stepped out into the warm September day. I dodged a few generic-looking shrubs around the perimeter of the faded yellow-brick building and stretched on my tiptoes near the first window. Thankfully, the shades were open so I could see inside with relative ease. The glare of the low-hanging September sun partly obstructed my view.

I cupped my hands around my eyes and squinted, trying to get a better look. I spotted a navy-blue couch, an oversized recliner, and a kitchen beyond that.

My perusal came to an abrupt stop, though.

What was that?

I pushed myself up farther on my toes, desperate to get a better look.

It couldn't be . . .

But it was.

Two legs stuck out on the other side of the couch. And an extremely long, scary tail poked out beside it.

PRANCED

I'd found the snake, but, unfortunately, it appeared to be too late.

Look for These Other Books in The Sierra Files:

Pounced (Book 1)

Animal-rights activist Sierra Nakamura never expected to stumble upon the dead body of a coworker while filming a project nor get involved in the investigation. But when someone threatens to kill her cats unless she hands over the "information," she becomes more bristly than an angry feline. Making matters worse is the fact that her cats—and the investigation—are driving a wedge between her and her boyfriend, Chad. With every answer she uncovers, old hurts rise to the surface and test her beliefs. Saving her cats might mean ruining everything else in her life. In the fight for survival, one thing is certain: either pounce or be pounced.

Hunted (Book 2)

Who knew a stray dog could cause so much trouble? Newlywed animal-rights activist Sierra Nakamura Davis must face her worst nightmare: breaking the news she eloped with Chad to her ultra-opinionated tiger mom. Her perfectionist parents have planned a vow-renewal ceremony at

Sierra's lush childhood home, but a neighborhood dog ruins the rehearsal dinner when it shows up toting what appears to be a fresh human bone. While dealing with the dog, a nosy neighbor, and an old flame turning up at the wrong times, Sierra hunts for answers. Her journey of discovery leads to more than just who committed the crime.

Pranced (Book 2.5, a Christmas novella)

Sierra Nakamura Davis thinks spending Christmas with her husband's relatives will be a real Yuletide treat. But when the animal-rights activist learns his family has a reindeer farm, she begins to feel more like the Grinch. Even worse, when Sierra arrives, she discovers the reindeer are missing. Sierra fears the animals might be suffering a worse fate than being used for entertainment purposes. Can Sierra set aside her dogmatic opinions to help get the reindeer home in time for the holidays? Or will secrets tear the family apart and ruin Sierra's dream of the perfect Christmas?

Rattled (Book 3)

"What do you mean a thirteen-foot lavender albino ball python is missing?" Tough-as-nails Sierra Nakamura Davis isn't one to get flustered. But trying to balance being a wife and a new mom with her crusade to help animals is proving harder than she imagined. Add a missing python, a high maintenance intern, and a dead body to the mix, and Sierra becomes the definition of rattled. Can she balance it all—and solve a possible murder—without losing her mind?

If you liked Pranced, you might like these books in the Squeaky Clean series:

Hazardous Duty (Book 1)

On her way to completing a degree in forensic science, Gabby St. Claire drops out of school and starts her own crime-scene cleaning business. When a routine cleaning job uncovers a murder weapon the police overlooked, she realizes that the wrong person is in jail. But the owner of the weapon is a powerful foe . . . and willing to do anything to keep Gabby quiet. With the help of her new neighbor, Riley Thomas, a man whose life and faith fascinate her, Gabby seeks to find the killer before another murder occurs.

Suspicious Minds (Book 2)

In this smart and suspenseful sequel to *Hazardous Duty*, crime-scene cleaner Gabby St. Claire finds herself stuck doing mold remediation to pay the bills. Her first day on the job, she uncovers a surprise in the crawlspace of a dilapidated home: Elvis, dead as a doornail and still wearing his blue-suede shoes. How could she possibly keep her nose out of a case like this?

CHRISTY BARRITT

It Came Upon a Midnight Crime (Book 2.5, a Novella)

Someone is intent on destroying the true meaning of Christmas—at least, destroying anything that hints of it. All around crime-scene cleaner Gabby St. Claire's hometown, anything pointing to Jesus as "the reason for the season" is being sabotaged. The crimes become more twisted as dismembered body parts are found at the vandalisms. Someone is determined to destroy Christmas . . . but Gabby is just as determined to find the Grinch and let peace on earth and goodwill prevail.

Organized Grime (Book 3)

Gabby St. Claire knows her best friend, Sierra, isn't guilty of killing three people in what appears to be an eco-terrorist attack. But Sierra has disappeared, her only contact a frantic phone call to Gabby proclaiming she's being hunted. Gabby is determined to prove her friend is innocent and to keep Sierra alive. While trying to track down the real perpetrator, Gabby notices a disturbing trend at the crime scenes she's cleaning, one that ties random crimes together—and points to Sierra as the guilty party. Just what has her friend gotten herself involved in?

Dirty Deeds (Book 4)

"Promise me one thing. No snooping. Just for one week." Gabby St. Claire knows that her fiancé's request is a simple one she should be able to honor. After all, Riley's law school reunion and attorneys' conference at a posh resort is a chance for them to get away from the mysteries Gabby often finds herself involved in as a crime-scene cleaner. Then an old friend of Riley's goes missing. Gabby suspects one of Riley's buddies might be behind the disappearance. When the missing woman's mom asks Gabby for help, how can she say no?

The Scum of All Fears (Book 5)

Gabby St. Claire is back to crime-scene cleaning and needs help after a weekend killing spree fills her work docket. A serial killer her fiancé put behind bars has escaped. His last words to Riley were: _I'll get out, and I'll get even_. Pictures of Gabby are found in the man's prison cell, messages are left for Gabby at crime scenes, someone keeps slipping in and out of her apartment, and her temporary assistant disappears. The search for answers becomes darker when Gabby realizes she's dealing with a criminal who is truly the scum of the earth. He will do anything to make Gabby's and Riley's lives a living nightmare.

To Love, Honor, and Perish (Book 6)

Just when Gabby St. Claire's life is on the right track, the unthinkable happens. Her fiancé, Riley Thomas, is shot and in life-threatening condition only a week before their wedding. Gabby is determined to figure out who pulled the trigger, even if investigating puts her own life at risk. As she digs deeper into the case, she discovers secrets better left alone. Doubts arise in her mind, and the one man with answers lies on death's doorstep. Then an old foe returns and tests everything Gabby is made of—physically, mentally, and spiritually. Will all she's worked for be destroyed?

Mucky Streak (Book 7)

Gabby St. Claire feels her life is smeared with the stain of tragedy. She takes a short-term gig as a private investigator—a cold case that's eluded detectives for ten years. The mass murder of a wealthy family seems impossible to solve, but Gabby brings more clues to light. Add to the mix a flirtatious client, travels to an exciting new city, and some quirky—albeit temporary—new sidekicks, and things get complicated. With every new development, Gabby prays that her "mucky streak" will end and the future will become clear. Yet every answer she uncovers leads her closer to danger—both for her life and for her heart.

Foul Play (Book 8)

Gabby St. Claire is crying "foul play" in every sense of the phrase. When the crime-scene cleaner agrees to go undercover at a local community theater, she discovers more than backstage bickering, atrocious acting, and rotten writing. The female lead is dead, and an old classmate who has staked everything on the musical production's success is about to go under. In her dual role of investigator and star of the show, Gabby finds the stakes rising faster than the opening-night curtain. She must face her past and make monumental decisions, not just about the play but also concerning her future relationships and career. Will Gabby find the killer before the curtain goes down—not only on the play, but also on life as she knows it?

Broom and Gloom (Book 9)

Gabby St. Claire is determined to get back in the saddle again. While in Oklahoma for a forensic conference, she meets her soon-to-be stepbrother, Trace Ryan, an up-and-coming country singer. A woman he was dating has disappeared, and he suspects a crazy fan may be behind it. Gabby agrees to investigate, as she tries to juggle her conference, navigate being alone in a new place, and locate a woman who may not want to be found. She discovers that sometimes taking life by the horns means staring danger in the face, no matter the consequences.

Dust and Obey (Book 10)

When Gabby St. Claire's ex-fiancé, Riley Thomas, asks for her help in investigating a possible murder at a couples retreat, she knows she should say no. She knows she should run far, far away from the danger of both being around Riley and the crime. But her nosy instincts and determination take precedence over her logic. Gabby and Riley must work together to find the killer. In the process, they have to confront demons from their past and deal with their present relationship.

Thrill Squeaker (Book 11)

An abandoned theme park. An unsolved murder. A decision that will change Gabby's life forever. Restoring an old amusement park and turning it into a destination resort seems like a fun idea for former crime-scene cleaner Gabby St. Claire. The side job gives her the chance to spend time with her friends, something she's missed since beginning a new career. The job turns out to be more than Gabby bargained for when she finds a dead body on her first day. Add to the mix legends of Bigfoot, creepy clowns, and ghostlike remnants of happier times at the park, and her stay begins to feel like a rollercoaster ride. Someone doesn't want the decrepit Mythical Falls to open again, but just how far is this person willing to go to ensure this venture fails? As the stakes rise and danger creeps closer, will Gabby be able to restore things in her own life that time has destroyed—including broken relationships? Or is her future closer to the fate of the doomed Mythical Falls?

***Swept Away*, a Honeymoon Novella (Book 11.5)**
Finding the perfect place for a honeymoon, away from any potential danger or mystery, is challenging. But Gabby's longtime love and newly minted husband, Riley Thomas, has done it. He has found a location with a nonexistent crime rate, a mostly retired population, and plenty of opportunities for relaxation in the warm sun. Within minutes of the newlyweds' arrival, a convoy of vehicles pulls up to a nearby house, and their honeymoon oasis is destroyed like a sandcastle in a

storm. Despite Gabby's and Riley's determination to keep to themselves, trouble comes knocking at their door—literally—when a neighbor is abducted from the beach directly outside their rental. Will Gabby and Riley be swept away with each other during their honeymoon . . . or will a tide of danger and mayhem pull them under?

Cunning Attractions (Book 12)

Politics. Love. Murder. Radio talk show host Bill McCormick is in his prime. He's dating a supermodel, his book is a bestseller, and his ratings have skyrocketed during the heated election season. But when Bill's ex-wife, Emma Jean, turns up dead, the media and his detractors assume the opinionated loudmouth is guilty of her murder. Bill's on-air rants about his demon-possessed ex don't help his case. Did someone realize that Bill was the perfect scapegoat? Or could Bill have silenced his Ice Queen ex once and for all? Gabby Thomas takes on the case, but she soon realizes that Emma Jean had too many enemies to count. From election conspiracy theories to scorned affections and hidden secrets, Emma Jean left a trail of trouble as her legacy. Gabby is determined to follow the twisted path until she finds answers.

While You Were Sweeping, a Riley Thomas Novella

Riley Thomas is trying to come to terms with life after a traumatic brain injury turned his world upside down. Away from everything familiar—including his crime-scene-cleaning former fiancée and his career as a social-rights attorney—he's determined to prove himself and regain his old life. But when he claims he witnessed his neighbor shoot and kill someone, everyone thinks he's crazy. When all evidence of the crime disappears, even Riley has to wonder if he's losing his mind.

Note: *While You Were Sweeping* is a spin-off mystery written in conjunction with the Squeaky Clean series featuring crime-scene cleaner Gabby St. Claire.

Holly Anna Paladin Mysteries:

Random Acts of Murder (Book 1)

When Holly Anna Paladin is given a year to live, she embraces her final days doing what she loves most—random acts of kindness. But one of her extreme good deeds goes horribly wrong, implicating her in a string of murders. Holly is suddenly thrust into a different kind of fight for her life. Could it also be random that the detective assigned to the case is her old high school crush and present-day nemesis? Will Holly find the killer before he ruins what is left of her life? Or will she spend her final days alone and behind bars?

Random Acts of Deceit (Book 2)

"Break up with Chase Dexter, or I'll kill him." Holly Anna Paladin never expected such a gut-wrenching ultimatum. With home invasions, hidden cameras, and bomb threats, Holly must make some serious choices. Whatever she decides, the consequences will either break her heart or break her soul. She tries to match wits with the Shadow Man, but the more she fights, the deeper she's drawn into the perilous situation. With her sister's wedding problems and the riots in the city, Holly has nearly reached her breaking point. She must stop this mystery man before someone she loves dies. But the deceit is threatening to pull her under . . . six feet under.

Random Acts of Malice (Book 3)
When Holly Anna Paladin's boyfriend, police detective Chase Dexter, says he's leaving for two weeks and can't give any details, she wants to trust him. But when she discovers Chase may be involved in some unwise and dangerous pursuits, she's compelled to intervene. Holly gets a run for her money as she's swept into the world of horseracing. The stakes turn deadly when a dead body surfaces and suspicion is cast on Chase. At every turn, more trouble emerges, making Holly question what she holds true about her relationship and her future. Just when she thinks she's on the homestretch, a dark horse arises. Holly might lose everything in a nail-biting fight to the finish.

Random Acts of Scrooge (Book 3.5)
Christmas is supposed to be the most wonderful time of the year, but a real-life Scrooge is threatening to ruin the season's good will. Holly Anna Paladin can't wait to celebrate Christmas with family and friends. She loves everything about the

season—celebrating the birth of Jesus, singing carols, and baking Christmas treats, just to name a few. But when a local family needs help, how can she say no? Holly's community has come together to help raise funds to save the home of Greg and Babette Sullivan, but a Bah-Humburgler has snatched the canisters of cash. Holly and her boyfriend, police detective Chase Dexter, team up to catch the Christmas crook. Will they succeed in collecting enough cash to cover the Sullivans' overdue bills? Or will someone succeed in ruining Christmas for all those involved?

Random Acts of Greed (Book 4)

Help me. Don't trust anyone. Do-gooder Holly Anna Paladin can't believe her eyes when a healthy baby boy is left on her doorstep. What seems like good fortune quickly turns into concern when blood spatter is found on the bottom of the baby carrier. Something tragic—maybe deadly—happened in connection with the infant. The note left only adds to the confusion. What does it mean by "Don't trust anyone"? Holly is determined to figure out the identity of the baby. Is his mom someone from the inner-city youth center where she volunteers? Or maybe the connection is through Holly's former job as a social worker? Even worse—what if the blood belongs to the baby's mom? Every answer Holly uncovers only leads to more questions. A sticky web of intrigue captures her imagination until she's sure of only one thing: she must protect the baby at all cost.

The Worst Detective Ever:

Ready to Fumble

I'm not really a private detective. I just play one on TV. Joey Darling, better known to the world as Raven Remington, detective extraordinaire, is trying to separate herself from her invincible alter ego. She played the spunky character for five years on the hit TV show Relentless, which catapulted her to fame and into the role of Hollywood's sweetheart. When her marriage falls apart, her finances dwindle to nothing, and her father disappears, Joey finds herself on the Outer Banks of North Carolina, trying to piece her life back together away from the limelight. A woman finds Raven—er, Joey—and insists on hiring her fictional counterpart to find a missing boyfriend. When someone begins staging crime scenes to match an episode of Relentless, Joey has no choice but to get involved.

Reign of Error

Sometimes in life, you just want to yell "Take two!" When a Polar Plunge goes terribly wrong and someone dies in the icy water, former TV detective Joey Darling wants nothing to do with subsequent investigation. But when her picture is found in the dead man's wallet and witnesses place her as the last person seen with the man, she realizes she's been cast in a role she never wanted: suspect. Joey makes the dramatic mistake of challenging the killer on camera, and now it's a race to find the bad guy before he finds her. Danger abounds and suspects are harder to find than the Lost Colony of Roanoke Island. But when Joey finds a connection with this case and the disappearance of her father, she knows there's no backing out. As hard as Joey tries to be like her super detective alter ego, the more things go wrong. Will Joey figure this one out? Or will her reign of error continue?

Safety in Blunders
(coming soon)

Carolina Moon Series:

Home Before Dark (Book 1)

Nothing good ever happens after dark. Country singer Daleigh McDermott's father often repeated those words. Now, her father is dead. As she's about to flee back to Nashville, she finds his hidden journal with hints that his death was no accident. Mechanic Ryan Shields is the only one who seems to believe Daleigh. Her father trusted the man, but her attraction to Ryan scares her. She knows her life and career are back in Nashville and her time in the sleepy North Carolina town is only temporary. As Daleigh and Ryan work to unravel the mystery, it becomes obvious that someone wants them dead. They must rely on each other—and on God—if they hope to make it home before the darkness swallows them.

Gone By Dark (Book 2)

Ten years ago, Charity White's best friend, Andrea, was abducted as they walked home from school. A decade later, when Charity receives a mysterious letter that promises answers, she returns to North Carolina in search of closure. With the help of her new neighbor, Police Officer Joshua Haven, Charity begins to track down mysterious clues concerning her friend's abduction. They soon discover that they must work together or both of them will be swallowed by the looming darkness.

Wait Until Dark (Book 3)

A woman grieving broken dreams. A man struggling to regain memories. A secret entrenched in folklore dating back two centuries. Antiquarian Felicity French has no clue the trouble she's inviting in when she rescues a man outside her grandma's old plantation house during a treacherous snowstorm. All she wants is to nurse her battered heart and wounded ego, as well as come to terms with her past. Now she's stuck inside with a stranger sporting an old bullet wound and forgotten hours. Coast Guardsman Brody Joyner can't remember why he was out in such perilous weather, how he injured his head, or how a strange key got into his pocket. He also has no idea why his pint-sized savior has such a huge chip on her shoulder. He has no choice but to make the best of things until the storm passes. Brody and Felicity's rocky start goes from tense to worse when danger closes in. Who else wants the mysterious key that somehow ended up in Brody's pocket? Why? The unlikely duo quickly becomes entrenched in an adventure of a lifetime, one that could have ties to local folklore and Felicity's ancestors. But sometimes the past leads to darkness . . . darkness that doesn't wait for anyone.

Light the Dark (a Christmas novella)

Nine months pregnant, Hope Solomon is on the run and fearing for her life. Desperate for warmth, food, and shelter, she finds what looks like an abandoned house. Inside, she discovers a Christmas that's been left behind—complete with faded decorations on a brittle Christmas tree and dusty stockings filled with loss. Someone spies smoke coming from the chimney of the empty house and alerts Dr. Luke Griffin, the owner. He rarely visits the home that harbors so many bittersweet memories for him. But no one is going to violate the space so near and dear to his heart. Then Luke meets Hope, and he knows this mother-to-be desperately needs help. With no room at any local inn, Luke invites Hope to stay, unaware of the danger following her. While running from the darkness, the embers of Christmas present are stirred with an unexpected birth and a holiday romance. But will Hope and Luke live to see a Christmas future?

Cape Thomas Series:

Dubiosity (Book 1)

Savannah Harris vowed to leave behind her old life as an investigative reporter. But when two migrant workers go missing, her curiosity spikes. As more eerie incidents begin afflicting the area, each works to draw Savannah out of her seclusion and raise the stakes—for her and the surrounding community. Even as Savannah's new boarder, Clive Miller, makes her feel things she thought long forgotten, she suspects he's hiding something too, and he's not the only one. As secrets emerge and danger closes in, Savannah must choose between faith and uncertainty. One wrong decision might spell the end . . . not just for her but for everyone around her. Will she unravel the mystery in time, or will doubt get the best of her?

Disillusioned (Book 2)

Nikki Wright is desperate to help her brother, Bobby, who hasn't been the same since escaping from a detainment camp run by terrorists in Colombia. Rumor has it that he betrayed his navy brothers and conspired with those who held him hostage, and both the press and the military are hounding him for answers. All Nikki wants is to shield her brother so he has time to recover and heal. But soon they realize the paparazzi are the least of their worries. When a group of men try to abduct Nikki and her brother, Bobby insists that Kade Wheaton, another former SEAL, can keep them out of harm's way. But can Nikki trust Kade? After all, the man who broke her heart eight years ago is anything but safe...Hiding out in a farmhouse on the Chesapeake Bay, Nikki finds her loyalties— and the remnants of her long-held faith—tested as she and Kade put aside their differences to keep Bobby's increasingly erratic behavior under wraps. But when Bobby disappears, Nikki will have to trust Kade completely if she wants to uncover the truth about a rumored conspiracy. Nikki's life—and the fate of the nation—depends on it.

Distorted (Book 3)
Coming soon

Standalones:

The Good Girl

Tara Lancaster can sing "Amazing Grace" in three harmonies, two languages, and interpret it for the hearing impaired. She can list the Bible canon backward, forward, and alphabetized. The only time she ever missed church was when she had pneumonia and her mom made her stay home. Then her life shatters and her reputation is left in ruins. She flees halfway across the country to dog-sit, but the quiet anonymity she needs isn't waiting at her sister's house. Instead, she finds a knife with a threatening message, a fame-hungry friend, a too-hunky neighbor, and evidence of . . . a ghost? Following all the rules has gotten her nowhere. And nothing she learned in Sunday School can tell her where to go from there.

Death of the Couch Potato's Wife (Suburban Sleuth Mysteries)

You haven't seen desperate until you've met Laura Berry, a career-oriented city slicker turned suburbanite housewife. Well-trained in the big-city commandment, "mind your own business," Laura is persuaded by her spunky seventy-year-old neighbor, Babe, to check on another neighbor who hasn't been seen in days. She finds Candace Flynn, wife of the infamous "Couch King," dead, and at last has a reason to get up in the morning. Someone is determined to stop her from digging deeper into the death of her neighbor, but Laura is just as determined to figure out who is behind the death-by-poisoned-pork-rinds.

Imperfect

Since the death of her fiancé two years ago, novelist Morgan Blake's life has been in a holding pattern. She has a major case of writer's block, and a book signing in the mountain town of Perfect sounds as perfect as its name. Her trip takes a wrong turn when she's involved in a hit-and-run: She hit a man, and he ran from the scene. Before fleeing, he mouthed the word "Help." First she must find him. In Perfect, she finds a small town that offers all she ever wanted. But is something sinister going on behind its cheery exterior? Was she invited as a guest of honor simply to do a book signing? Or was she lured to town for another purpose—a deadly purpose?

The Gabby St. Claire Diaries: a tween mystery series

The Curtain Call Caper (Book 1)

Is a ghost haunting the Oceanside Middle School auditorium? What else could explain the disasters surrounding the play—everything from missing scripts to a falling spotlight and damaged props? Seventh-grader Gabby St. Claire has dreamed about being part of her school's musical, but a series of unfortunate events threatens to shut down the production. While trying to uncover the culprit and save her fifteen minutes of fame, she also has to manage impossible teachers, cliques, her dysfunctional family, and a secret she can't tell even her best friend. Will Gabby figure out who or what is sabotaging the show . . . or will it be curtains for her and the rest of the cast?

The Disappearing Dog Dilemma (Book 2)

Why are dogs disappearing around town? When two friends ask seventh-grader Gabby St. Claire for her help in finding their missing canines, Gabby decides to unleash her sleuthing skills to sniff out whoever is behind the act. But time management and relationships get tricky as worrisome weather, a part-time job, and a new crush interfere with Gabby's investigation. Will her determination crack the case? Or will shadowy villains, a penchant for overcommitting, and even her own heart put her in the doghouse?

The Bungled Bike Burglaries (Book 3)

Stolen bikes and a long-forgotten time capsule leave one amateur sleuth baffled and busy. Seventh-grader Gabby St. Claire is determined to bring a bike burglar to justice—and not just because mean girl Donabell Bullock is strong-arming her. But each new clue brings its own set of trouble. As if that's not enough, Gabby finds evidence of a decades-old murder within the contents of the time capsule, but no one seems to take her seriously. As her investigation heats up, will Gabby's knack for being in the wrong place at the wrong time with the wrong people crack the case? Or will it prove hazardous to her health?

About the Author:

USA Today has called Christy Barritt's books "scary, funny, passionate, and quirky."

Christy writes both mystery and romantic suspense novels that are clean with underlying messages of faith. Her books have won the Daphne du Maurier Award for Excellence in Suspense and Mystery, have been twice nominated for the Romantic Times' Reviewers' Choice Award, and have finaled for both a Carol Award and Foreword Magazine's Book of the Year.

She's married to her Prince Charming, a man who thinks she's hilarious--but only when she's not trying to be. Christy's a self-proclaimed klutz, an avid music lover who's known for spontaneously bursting into song, and a road trip aficionado.

When she's not working or spending time with her family, she enjoys singing, playing the guitar, and exploring small, unsuspecting towns where people have no idea how accident prone she is.

Find Christy online at:
www.christybarritt.com
www.facebook.com/christybarritt
www.twitter.com/cbarritt

Sign up for Christy's newsletter to get information

on all of her latest releases here:
www.christybarritt.com/newsletter-sign-up/

If you enjoyed this book, please consider leaving a review.

Made in United States
Orlando, FL
06 February 2024